Brothers of the Night

BROTHERS OF THE NIGHT

GAY VAMPIRE STORIES

edited by Michael Rowe

and Thomas S. Roche

CLEIS
PRESS

Published in the United States by Cleis Press Inc., P.O. Box 14684, San Francisco, California 94114.
Printed in the United States.

Book design and production: Pete Ivey
Cover photograph: Phyllis Christopher
Cover model: Vince Constabileo
Cleis logo art: Juana Alicia

First Edition.
10 9 8 7 6 5 4 3 2 1

All works are used with permission of the authors. "Old World Manners" © 1997 by Bruce Benderson. "Angel Baby" © 1997 by Michael Thomas Ford. "Superheroes" © 1997 by Caitlín R. Kiernan. "The Nightwatch Is a Lonely Vigil" © 1997 by Kevin Andrew Murphy. "The Whole Vampire Thing" © 1997 by Ron Oliver. "Forever October" © 1997 by David Quinn. "Board Center 4 Car Train" © 1997 by Thomas S. Roche. "The Dead of Winter" © 1997 by Michael Rowe. "Amsterdam" © 1997 by Simon Sheppard. "Third Night" © 1997 by Robert Thomson. "Letting Go" © 1997 by Edo van Belkom.

Library of Congress Cataloging-in-Publication Data

Brothers of the night : gay male vampire stories / edited by Michael Rowe and Thomas S. Roche. -- 1st ed.
    p. cm.
    ISBN 1-57344-025-6 (paper)
    1. Vampires--Fiction. 2. Horror tales, American. 3. Gay men--Fiction. 4. American Fiction--20th century. I. Rowe, Michael, 1962–   . II. Roche, Thomas S.
PS648.V35B76 1997
813'.087380835206642--dc21

"And you, their best beloved one, are now to me, flesh of my flesh; blood of my blood; kin of my kin; my bountiful wine-press for awhile; and shall be later on my companion and my helper...now you shall come to my call. When my brain says "Come!" to you, you shall cross land or sea to do my bidding; and to that end this!"
— Bram Stoker, *Dracula*

For Randy Murphy
— Michael Rowe

I could live a little there
In the midst of the light
When the darkness closed in
I could have broke down and cried
— Joy Division, "She's Lost Control"

For Alex
hang in there baby
— Thomas Roche

Contents

ACKNOWLEDGMENTS

The editors would like to once again thank Felice Newman and Frédérique Delacoste of Cleis Press for their ongoing support. Thanks to Phyllis Christopher for the cover photo and to Pete Ivey for the design. Finally, thank you to the writers for giving their best work for this volume, and for helping set a new standard for the vampire genre.

Michael Rowe would like to acknowledge his muse, Marcus MacDonald, an incubus so superbly male, so magnificently larger-than-life, that he is best appreciated either in the context of a grand Romantic friendship or within the pages of a vampyre tale. He also acknowledges the friendship of Tasia Hazisavvas. For the beauty of his art and the gift of his friendship, he thanks James Huctwith. Lastly, most importantly, he thanks his post-nuclear family—his life-partner Brian McDermid, and Shaw Madson—for their love and support.

Thomas Roche would like to thank all the people who supported the first book, especially the folks at Boadecia's and Dark Carnival in Berkeley, and Modern Times, Good Vibrations, and A Different Light in San Francisco. Thanks to Clint Catalyst and Roderick's Chamber for welcoming creatures of the night. Thanks to Bill Brent for helping Phyllis and me with the cover shoot. Finally, he sends gracious thanks to all the brothers of the night who darkened his life and haunted his dangerous midnights.

INTRODUCTION

In Anne Rice's introduction to *Interview With The Vampire*—a film with a deeply homoerotic undercurrent, no matter what anyone says—the author and screenwriter says that the film upon which her novel is based isn't "just about vampires," it's really about "us."

Well, *Brothers of the Night* is really about vampires. That's precisely *why* it's about us.

For the vampire's story, like our own stories, celebrates the erotic power of ritual bloodletting—even, and perhaps especially, in a cultural landscape blasted by AIDS and social alienation. Our first collection of gay vampire stories, *Sons of Darkness: Tales of Men, Blood and Immortality* (Cleis Press, 1996) made the homoerotic content of the vampire myth quite explicit:

> Perhaps the vampire remembers a time when it was different: when he could hunt, drunk with power, knowing that his immortality was assured by that very lust for blood that drove him, knowing that the ecstasy of that forbidden draught would keep his heart beating long after the priests and their faithful had consigned his soul to God. Those glorious nights may seem over. But for those who crave blood, and whose craving sustains them through a thousand midnights, these nights of passion can never be over. As long as the moon shines, the blood lust will rise again.

The vampire is queer, by definition. It is no accident that the public's fascination with vampires has always peaked at times of shifting sexuality and growing conservatism: In repressive Victorian England was born Count Dracula; the paranoid and depressed 1930s, following the decadent and sensualist 1920s, were haunted by the vampire films of Universal Pictures, and by Bela Lugosi, who will forever serve as film's defining vampire. The conservative and (in the United States) McCarthy-badgered late 1950s brought Hammer Studio's Horror of Dracula, and its many sequels rode the wave of newfound sexual permissiveness, the women's movement, lesbian and gay rights, the countercultural youth movements, and everything else that the 1960s had to offer. Now, of course, in the age of AIDS and the sex-phobia it has engendered, comes a revival of gothic culture and a widespread interest in vampires.

Lesbian themes are common in contemporary horror fiction and movies. But work involving male homoeroticism is rare in horror, being largely limited to tales of gay male serial killers and psychopaths with father-fixations. Certainly this has begun to change in recent years, and books like *Sons of Darkness* and *Brothers of the Night* are certainly forging new ground, which is an intoxicating opportunity.

Brothers of the Night presents powerful stories in which raw male sexuality and raw terror are subtly intertwined. We have tried to select stories that draw as much from gothic horror fiction —contemporary as well as classic—and from archetypes of classic vampire movies as they do from popular gay writing.

Bruce Benderson's own personal themes of addiction and social stigma are reflected in the mirror of European class structure in "Old World Manners." In Michael Thomas Ford's "Angel Baby" a murderously ravenous child becomes the symbol of his mother's attraction to the homoerotic ritual in which he was conceived. Ron Oliver once again returns to image- and youth-obsessed Hollywood—from which so many vampires have sprung—and wryly turns L.A.'s facade on its head. In "Third Night" by Robert Thomson, we see the terror and sensuous wonder of anticipation as a soon-to-be vampire nears the third night of his transformation. Simon Sheppard's "Amsterdam" paints a portrait of loneliness in that international city of indulgence. The suburban teenagers in Caitlín R. Kiernan's "Superheroes" graduate from *The Rocky Horror Picture Show*, one of the most important queer movies of all times, to their own real live horror story. In "The Nightwatch is a Lonely Vigil," Kevin Murphy explores what it means to be a knight...and to love one. David Quinn's "Forever October" engages us in the delusions of a blood-obsessed protgonist who re-visits his first desire at his twentieth high school reunion. In "Letting Go," Edo van Belkom embraces death as a way through the grieving process. Finally, the editors offer you their own versions of the vampire mythos—Rowe in a traditional, sensuous tale of vampiric seduction and the terror of midnight hunger, Roche with his story of a burnout punk predator exiled by his addiction to the badlands under a blasted city, forever searching for redemption and forever betrayed by his hunger.

We hope that you will appreciate the power and the beauty of these brothers of the night. They will tempt you and seduce you. But don't think for a moment that that seduction is benign, for malignancy is part and parcel of the predator's existence. The vampire comes to you with open arms, inviting you into his dark embrace—but, Brother, think twice—this is not a love story. The vampire craves your blood.

And, Brother...he shall have it.

—Michael Rowe and Thomas S. Roche
August 1997

Brothers of the Night

THIRD NIGHT

ROBERT THOMSON

He came to me through shadows and gray, through cold and stench and diffused light, the fog of a wet dream. He appeared as my darkest secret and became my only need. He became flesh from desire and has left me wondering what will happen to me, how much of my body will be taken over by him, and how much of the blood and souls of others I will need to survive, and what will remain of me.

I am almost his now, almost completely. In the past two nights he has seen me through the stages, wiped my brow of sweat and my chest of vomit, bathed me in tubs of steaming water and dried me as I shivered beneath his firm hands. I've been rejecting food since the first night. My hunger for it has waned and in its place an incredible thirst has risen. I didn't know that first night what it was I wanted. Tonight, the third night, I know.

Hours after he drank from me, he poured water from a ceramic cup into my mouth. I felt it trickle down my parched throat, which rasped when I took a breath. After I rose on the second night he told me I would no longer be able to accept water as a means of rehydrating my internal organs which, by his account, were going through a rapid and complicated metamorphosis. Tonight, he said, water would not nourish me. Tonight, he said, everything would change. And he gave a half smile and placed his hand on my chest, where my heart is—or was. It was barely beating, he said. It was almost time. He would not drink from me again.

Thrice already now he has punctured my neck and taken from me what he needs. I saw the dull sheen on his incisors as his lips parted and he descended on me, holding my arms back ever so lightly and managing a reassuring air, as if administering a foul-tasting medicine that would make me well. I cannot say I resisted him. I cannot say I detest him for what he's done, although he has destroyed everything I once knew. But he has given to me in its place a magnificent promise, an eternal promise, and I knew from his cool, shallow eyes he would not lie. I felt his lips moving lightly over the holes in my throat and through the haze of red that filled his eyes I sensed his determination, as if he could see past all this harsh business and was focusing on a clearer picture, when things wouldn't be so trying, when our bodies would be in synch and our minds connected as though one. Soon, he said. Soon.

Even before I had seen him, he spoke to me. *Rid yourself of all your human desires. Reach for any and all experiences that pique your interest.* He told me to live quickly, for he was coming. And even though I only heard the words in the chambers of my thoughts, I knew they were coming from him, just as I knew what his face would look like, how the texture of his skin would feel when he finally pressed himself against me, so cool and supple, how I would feel tiny explosions in my temples that would ripple and course and throb down to my pelvis. In the nights before he came I touched myself at the height of ecstasy and felt someone else's hands guiding me, felt the wisps of my hair being shifted by another's deep breathing, felt his breath, his hands, caressing me, preparing me. He came to me, time and again, through my lonely dreams. I sometimes manage to convince myself that I in fact created him and that I alone can destroy him. But the weight of reality pulls on me each time I've tried to rise from the bed these past few evenings just to walk to the window and look out. His strength within me binds me to the bed, keeps me rapt with attention when I hear footsteps in the hall—his footsteps—and numbs me when I shake and lose control and cannot be held, cannot be controlled, cannot be sent back to the time before him. So if I have indeed created him, then by destroying him I would destroy myself, for my need of him is absolute. His intervention was inevitable, his incitement unnecessary, his involvement inexorable. We are no longer separate.

Only two weeks ago these notions would have made me laugh. I would have scoffed at any thoughts of men in black cloaks walking, unstoppable, through rain and dense fog to get to me and take from me. That a man's eyes could hold me spellbound, suspend my own will and cause me to doubt myself was unthinkable. And the thought of wanting this, to submit and subvert and be taken by a man—and wanting a man— was reprehensible and blasphemous to me. Yet here I am in this dark swirling fog with only his eyes to guide me, and I am more than contented, more that satisfied.

"I've been waiting for you," I told him when my eyes finally beheld him. He gave a nod and motioned for me to follow him.

"And I have been waiting for you."

His is a noble face, a distinguished visage with dark gray eyes tinged with red, and lips cool and kissable. We walked in silence, although I could hear him speaking to me, his thoughts my own. We came upon a place where he stopped and raised his arm to slow me. He put his hand to my cheek and looked into my eyes. He had need of me—and not merely for food, this he told me the next night I met him. I would be well cared for and would never be wanting. He promised.

"These strange ways," I heard him saying, "are new to me and I should like a companion, an accomplice, if you will." I could only imagine his sensuous lips at my throat and elsewhere, his long, elegant fingers bracing me, the weight of him against me and the dozens of questions I would ask him. Later, he told me, later.

On that second meeting we went to my apartment. He looked about thoughtfully and then sat himself on the sofa.

"Are you willing to leave this?"

Of course. "Where will you be taking me?"

"Everywhere."

"Will I become like you?"

"Yes."

"You have a spell on me, don't you?"

"Think of it not as a spell, but as a power. It is my will."

"And if I become like you, will I have this power?"

"In time," he said, "it will be yours." He raised his arm and extended his hand toward me. "Give me your hand." I did what he said.

He took my hand in his and held it there. His hand was strong and cool. I became aroused. He smiled at me, a knowing, wise smile. His other hand went to my chest. He rubbed me gently. I thought I would faint or combust from wanting him.

"I will come back in two nights. Think about what I've said tonight. Think about how you feel. Be ready in two days. If you are not ready I will find you and drink from you and leave you to die. If you are ready we will have your things brought to my home, you will accompany me, and I will make you as I am."

"And what do you call yourself? What are you?"

He did not laugh as he should have at such a question. I could feel the restraints of his power over me waning, and I panicked. He rose from the couch, looked deeply into my eyes, and spoke simply.

"I am the soil beneath your feet, the moon in the sky, the air in your lungs. I am all that came before you: knowledge, fear, insanity, and wealth, and I am what is to follow. I am the victim and the conqueror and the force that drives the tide. Everything and nothing, I am." He moved to the window and stopped. "Two nights. Think on it. Find and follow your need." And with that he had gone.

That night I dreamt of fire and rain, emaciated bodies lurching through icy cold, their gnarled fingers reaching out toward me, their blistered mouths crying out words and sounds I could not hear through the layers of consciousness that separated us. I woke with a start, sat upright in bed, my pulse racing, my penis erect, perspiration dampening my forehead and feeling certain that I had been warned. A strange sensation, or rather a thought, appeared: I knew that I would be going someplace and that I had no control over my journey. As I settled back down in bed I pondered briefly my situation and wondered whether this dark man controlled my fate. Perhaps he was exactly what he said he was, the force that drives the tide, everything and nothing. It was then that I knew this man had no control over fate. He *was* fate.

The next two days passed like a cloud obscuring the sun. I found myself writing letters to people I saw almost every week. I gave my notice to my landlord, went to see M at a crumbling repertory cinema, had sex in the park, had sex again in my kitchen, and then again, with a third man in his bedroom at his mother's home while she slept in the next room. He kissed me one moment then turned away from me the instant he had climaxed. I dressed and left, feeling nothing in particular except a longing for the dark man's hands on me and the feeling of cool, dry night air.

The afternoon before he returned I visited my parents' grave and left a bouquet of cheap flowers between their tombstones. I closed my bank account and purchased a beautiful, long black coat and a pair of expensive sunglasses. Returning to my apartment I took a long bath and then waited for him to arrive. I don't know when I fell asleep; it could have been any time after ten o'clock. I was awakened by a knock at the door. I sat up from the couch and looked at my watch. Two minutes after midnight.

He looked at me quizzically when I opened the door.

"Come in."

"Am I interrupting your sleep?" he asked.

"I didn't know when to expect you...."

"Have you thought about what I've offered you?"

"Can't you read my thoughts? Wasn't it you who made me dream those dreams the night you left me?"

He entered the apartment, passing me as if I weren't even there.

"I am not responsible for the thoughts that enter your mind," he said. "With the exception of relaying my thoughts to you, my powers are influential at best. Thus the desire you feel, your curiosity, the pull toward me. These are all things I can influence. I cannot, however, change your mind."

"I don't believe you."

"But you believe in me," he said, almost a question.

"Yes," I answered.

"That much I knew," he whispered, drawing his hand to my cheek and stroking it. "For it is obvious. Your desires are not as subtlely hidden as you think. And no, I do not read minds. I sense vibrations, I feel changes in people's body language and chemistry. I am aware of many things of which you are not. For instance, I am aware of your readiness but I can also sense your repulsion. This dichotomy is something you've dealt with before in your life, around your sexuality, perhaps."

I felt myself moving away. His voice echoed and resounded as meaningless noise in my ears. I felt a wave of uncertainty rush through me, causing my legs to tremble and my eyes to search the room.

"Will you allow me to take you so you can be with me?"

I shook my head. No sound escaped my lips. I felt sweat dampening my hairline. He moved closer to me. I stepped back and bumped into the sofa.

"Not many men are presented with the opportunity of deciding their own fate. You remember your choices? Do you think you're being wise?"

"Leave me," I stammered, fighting and hating myself for wanting him. "Find someone else."

"But there is no one else," he grinned at me. And before I could move or think or scream or turn away, he was upon me, gazing into my eyes, into me, through me. His hands placed on either side of my head pulled me back, exposing my neck. I felt the veins move closer to my skin, the blood rushing faster, the saliva rising in the back of my throat, the chill of one of his rings against my scalp. I saw his eyes open, his lips part. Light from somewhere in the room, or possibly from outside—a streetlight, a neon light—flashed upon his sharp teeth as he bent forward, pulling toward me, in and out of control. I felt his mouth on my neck. His lips opened, his tongue on my skin, moving about, arousing me, bracing me, warming and enticing me. He pulled in close to me, his body tight against mine, his mouth on my throat, his thigh pressing against my erection, his hands holding my head still and his fingers lightly massaging it at the same time. He trembled a second, a rush of apprehension, perhaps, swirled his tongue in a moist circle on my neck and then hesitated for a mere heartbeat. And then he opened me. I felt the tear of his teeth piercing my flesh, the tearing away, the sharp, sweet pain and then heard the sucking sound as he drank from me, took my blood and began emptying me. A flash of white eclipsed my vision. My knees buckled; he caught and held me, his arms moving around my waist as the sucking continued. I began to feel lighter. The pain died away. As he pulled back I could feel his tongue licking the wounds he had made. He moved back and gently helped me slide onto the couch.

"I did want it," I managed in a hoarse whisper. "Help me, won't you?"

Of course he would.

The next night he appeared at my window. I merely moved as if to go open it and he was inside, instantly wrapping his arms around me and nuzzling his head into the curve of my neck and soon filling my ears with sucking noises and the sweet, dying pain and wavering light.

I passed the next twenty-four hours in a daze. It seemed like only minutes before he reappeared and moved my head to the side so he could examine my neck.

"This is the last time," he said. "If you still want to join me, I will drink from you again and in three nights you will walk as I walk. If you prefer, I can let you die."

With what little strength I had left, I removed the shirt I was wearing and went to him, my head tilted to the side, offering myself to him, desperately wanting to be taken away from the aching void in which I'd been living for the past two days.

"You are delicious," he said in a gruff voice as his lips met the skin of my neck and he swirled his tongue along the surface before breaking the skin and sucking my blood out of me. I don't remember anything past that point.

I fell into a dream of sensations and shadows; the feel of his teeth gliding into me, breaking open my skin and moving about the torn flesh;

wisps of fog cut with moonlight or rays from a streetlamp moving about my mind like a bright, lost cloud.

I became conscious sometime later. He had wrapped me in a blanket and rooted me in a tight space. Somehow in my blackout he had transported me to his house. I woke with a scream, beating my fists against the thick wood that encased me. My noise soon woke him. I heard the sliding of wood. A crack of light appeared above me which soon widened. I saw his face lit with evening shades. He looked at me seriously, without pity or concern, and said something I cannot recall. He lifted me out of the sleeping chamber—a flat box not unlike a coffin, but larger—and carried me to a bed.

"Your first night will be the most difficult," he told me, wiping my brow. "I will help you."

The second night was just a blur of convulsions and agony.

And now, on the third night, as I rise from my sleeping chamber I hear the wind thrashing against the house and thunder off in the distance. I cross the room halfway and stop beside his sleeping chamber to give it a gentle knock. I want him to rise and to look at me and to smile. To say it's good and that he is glad. But he is still inside. I rap again, my knuckles hard against the wooden cabinet. I become aware of something as I open the lid of his chamber and find it empty. Perhaps he has already risen. Maybe that's him I sense behind me now. I spin around and find a stern-faced woman in a dark gray suit standing in the doorway.

"What are you doing here?" she hisses. Before I can answer, she steps quickly toward me, backing me against the wall. "Why have you come here?" Her eyebrows arch. Hot sour breath from her mouth. Her skin pale. "Get out." She leans in toward me, her eyes moving from my face to my neck. She tilts her head and then lets out a scream so filled with pain and shock it frightens me. But she stops abruptly, looks about the room quickly and then back to my face. One of her hands rises to my face. She pulls my mouth open by lifting my upper lip up roughly. She freezes. I can feel her breath on my face, her hand holding my lip up, a shift in her energy. Slowly, shaking her head in tiny movements from side to side, she steps back, unpinning me from the cold brick wall.

"He has made you as he is. I can tell by your eyes and your teeth that you are finished."

"Where is he?" I ask, and hearing the panic in my own voice startles me. "Who are you?"

"Your master has left for Europe," she says in a satisfied voice.

"Europe?" I repeat.

"Yes."

"But why? He didn't tell me....When will he be back?"

She moves further away from me and closes the lid to his sleeping chamber. "In a month, perhaps. I am Mary, his servant," she says, smiling. "I shall attend to your needs in his absence."

"But what am I to do? He just left?"

"I can bring someone to you this evening sir, if that's what your concern is."

"How do you know about all of this?"

"That is a story that would take years to unravel. Perhaps it's just best to say that you are very safe trusting me." She moves back into the center of the room, holding her hands together in front of her.

"I have something for you here," she gestures with her hands. "It's a gift I know your master would like you to have."

"What is it?" I am not entirely unsuspicious.

She moves one hand away, raises the other toward me, and reveals a silver cross, no larger than one of her fingers. I feel an instant trembling in my temples. She jumps toward me, pressing the object into my face, searing me, burning my flesh. I cry out and sweep her hand to the side with my arm. The shiny cross flies to the floor. Mary moves to pick it up, but my pain has given me strength and I stop her, grabbing her by the waist and pulling her to me. With one of my hands pulling her arm and the other around her waist, I spin us around and throw her into the wall. I hear her face hit the brick. She is stunned, perhaps, but does not collapse.

The next thing I feel are her fingernails slashing across my cheek. She shrieks as she does it. I feel heat on my face and then nothing. Wrestling with her, I manage to throw her onto the floor. Her legs flail about, sometimes landing well-placed kicks, but I don't feel it anymore. I don't care. I only see one thing, feel one thing. And it's coursing throughout her body, only inches away.

Sitting on top of her, I place my hands on her head in an attempt to hold her as still as possible. I twist her head to the side, revealing the expanse of her neck. She screams and cries. I move in closer, and whisper into her ear, "He's mine now." She utters a little whimper of protest before I tilt my head downward and open my mouth.

She screams as I enter her, my teeth piercing the flesh of her neck. I can feel the shift of muscles and veins against the softness of my lips as she screams. If I weren't sucking I would be smiling. Revenge is sweeter than blood.

The scream subsides and I feel her move a little bit. Her arm is fumbling about, twitching perhaps. I continue sucking, my eyes roaming about, but my vision is obscured by her head. And then I feel it again, the odd stab of pain in my temples. I pause and then feel Mary moving slightly once more. Then she is still. I continue drinking.

I feel a warmth coming at me, feel it on my forehead. A blistering heat rises and flashes from out of nowhere. I feel the physical sensation of fire on my forehead. Her hand looms above me, presses into me, the shiny silver cross glides toward me. She plants it on the skin of my forehead.

My mouth closes shut, pinching a fold of the skin of her neck between my teeth. I scream internally, pulling one arm up to knock hers away from my face and then pull my head up and over at the same time. I give a swift, long tug at her neck and feel the tense resistance in my mouth. I tug again ferociously, ripping layers of flesh from her neck. The cross falls to the floor, covered with blood. A six-inch piece of torn, bloody flesh hangs from my mouth. In the dark of the room I look down and see her mangled throat. I feel nothing but a subsiding rage. And a need for him.

Blood seeps from the hole I have left in her neck. It spittles and excretes with decreasing speed and intensity. Blood has pooled beneath her, in a puddle, and has soaked through my clothing, covered my arms and hands. I can feel it on my cheeks, in my hair, on my mouth, trickling down my chest, surging through my body, waking me and bringing me back to life.

I pull myself away from her. I stand up, wipe my mouth of blood. I go to the doorway and open the heavy wooden door. I step through it and down the steps and outside into the night.

OLD WORLD MANNERS

BRUCE BENDERSON

A DRUG addict and alcoholic, fresh out of several years in the worst, most derelict bars imaginable, I was determined once and for all to put an end to my downward spiral. Because my favorite addiction had been crack, I knew that even the most insignificant word or image could start the chain of associations going—an energy synapse series with a conductive will of its own.

"Smoke," "match," "rock," the sight of an unbent wire hanger like the one I had habitually used to dig out my stem, a certain odor, or an inkling of police presence on the street, suddenly took on a kind of fetishized eroticism, bringing me back to the past where the close air of a sealed-off room, the isolation of out-of-date pop music, and occasional voice-overs from a TV left carelessly on, all contributed to the heightened atmosphere of onanism.

Crack stem in hand, I had seen time telescope into a jagged series of arousals and climaxes, keeping me close to an endless and ecstatic state of orgasmic disintegration. Such continual masturbation, aided at times by a videotape or an underclass male prostitute, but often spurred purely by a cascading imagination, was fueled by frequent inhalations from the pipe. And only when the last rock had melted into smoke did the crawling, searching nightmare for more of the life substance descend upon me with all its horror. Then consciousness was compacted into a ghoulish struggle, as each gesture became fraught with imminent failure, and life slipped through my fingers like sand through the hand of a skeleton.

As time went on, even continual inhalations could not delay the encroachment of time. A tide of dying swallowed me with maddening slowness. It wasn't long before I subjected myself to recovery. I was aware that the public testimonies and self-accounting of the recovery process owed much to Luther, so I prepared myself to deal with this contemporary form of conversion. Repulsive as the process was, I swallowed my distaste and gave myself up to the repetitive spiritual biographies designed to break down defenses and make me surrender.

Within a year I felt confident enough to return to normal life. I had planned to take up again the profession of scholar, which I'd abandoned for almost a decade in favor of my addictions. Fortunately, I'd chanced upon an unusual opportunity. A disabled French scholar whose name had meant a great deal to me in my youthful academic days had placed a small ad in a journal asking for an assistant. He was a specialist in a certain *fin de siecle* writer known for his decadent excesses and for a later zealous conversion to conservative Catholicism. Within a week my letter had been answered, and arrangements were made for my voyage to the French Alps.

IT was in the mountains, fifty miles from Grenoble, that the Professor had been sent for a lengthy, perhaps terminal, convalescence. The tumor that had shrunk him to skeletal proportions had not responded to treatment and had spread to the rest of his body. Wracked by toothaches and migraines, the famous scholar of the infamous yellow-book writer found himself following in the footsteps to Calvary of the man who had been the object of his lifetime of study. For that man had himself spent his last years in excruciating pain and as an oblate of a monastery.

This mirroring process was merely one phase of a perhaps infinite progression in which I was about to partake. Consider that the writer who was the subject of my soon-to-be employer's study had himself emulated medieval sages, among them the formidable monster Gilles de Rais. After his treatise on Gilles de Rais, the writer had undergone an intense religious conversion, although his pious impulses had taken on a sumptuous tinge that could have been described as lurid. As in the work of the late medieval artist Matthias Grunewald, whose paintings never ceased to fascinate the convert, the drama of fall and redemption beckoned because it promised more grisly and bloodthirsty images and scenarios. To make matters worse, while in the prime of his talents, the writer was afflicted with unbearable pain in the region of the mouth. and eventually discovered that he was suffering from terminal oral cancer. Thus did the writer, and, almost a century later, his most devoted scholar, suffer very similar fates.

WITH a pounding heart I swerved through the mute landscape of rock, grass, and patches of snow up a peak close to Mount Blanc, whose razor silhouette could actually be glimpsed from time to time through the crab apple trees. A wind seemed to explode their blossoms from the branches, spraying them against my windshield. The exhilaration I felt for the first time since my addiction reawakened the hope that I had not broken all libidinous ties to nature but could once again vigorously partake in the pleasures of the sensual world.

Soon I reached the peak and the sanitarium housed in a former monastery, staffed by nuns. As I was shown to a small white cell with a cot, wash basin, and writing desk, instructed to appear at meals promptly, and handed a schedule of events that included meditation, the sinking realization came upon me that being a visitor of the sick, I would be expected to enter their austere code. Here illnesses of all persuasions, from cancer to AIDS, were reduced in theory to the same context of original sin, and no one questioned the sick person's duty—or right—to the correct, nearly silent life of the penitent. The kinds of discussions that tend to establish hierarchies among humans weren't considered seemly here, as all had reached the same terminal stage.

With these sobering thoughts in mind, I was brought in to the Professor, an emaciated man with wispy, transparent hair and an inflamed, peeling face. Pulling himself up from a carved wooden chair by means of a cane, he extended a shrunken hand. He was, he said, anxious to take a ride down the mountain up which I had just come, and without so much as another word, he struggled from the room, signaling me to follow. We were intercepted by one of the nuns, who in angry, cautionary tones reminded him that the obligatory luncheon was about to be served and went so far as to lead us away from our path into the dining room. She barely was able to look into the Professor's face, seeming to find some kind of unholy terror in the sight of his emaciation.

At the rows of white-clothed tables sat the patients and guests in a cocoon of discretion and decrepitude. Our frugal meal consisted of a tolerable red wine, soup, a thin, unsalted root puree, some steamed fish, and macaroni covered with a bèchamel that I declined. The plates were brought by waiters in black trousers and white jackets, whose crisp service seemed yet another kind of discipline for both patient and staff. Opposite me sat a woman, whose sight had been affected by a tumor, and her daughter, a teenager whose blank expression didn't mask her frustration in being helpless to do something for her mother. Having been told that I was an American, the mother released a small cascade of good English after which we began to eat in silence. The Professor took a spoonful of the soup, seemed not to be able to swallow it, and gave up. I brought the gruel to my lips, hyperconscious of the sound of each spoon touching its plate.

WHEN, after a dispute between the Professor and the same nun, we were finally allowed to begin our afternoon drive, my employer was bundled into his Scottish shawl by another mute nun and pushed toward the exit in a wooden wheelchair. We moved briskly across the polished floor of the dim corridor, broken at regular lengths by squares of harsh light. When we had burst outside into an even harsher blaze of sun, his voice rose into an excited rasp:

"I hope you won't mind including my little friend in our downward jaunt!" The words were an incantation. A scruffy local of about thirteen jumped suddenly onto our path. He had a flattened, feline snout and a big, impudent smile that would have looked like a leer on an older person. The nun gasped, let go of the wheelchair, and dove back into the old monastery, while the boy grabbed the wheelchair with dirty, callused hands and trotted away with it.

At the car, the boy lifted the frail Professor out of the wheelchair and into his wiry arms. There was a wolfish gleam of content in the professor's eyes as he gazed with happy familiarity at the boy, who seemed, surprisingly enough, to return the look impishly. The boy placed him on the front seat, then hopped into the back without a word. I snatched a quick, rather annoyed look at his lanky frame, took in his black hair, which was thick and peltish, and his flawless skin, which was so pale that the circles under his mean-looking almond-shaped eyes looked blue. His famished cheeks formed two shadows over a gleaming, impudent mouth and a tiny pink tongue that nervously kept it lubricated.

I wondered if he were a peasant from further down the mountain. The stains on his rolled-cuff woolens had to be mud, or manure; and those tiny pinprick scratches on his neck and forearms were probably from field work.

THE air became heavier and the light denser as I steered the car down the spiral of the mountain road, waiting for my employer to broach the subject of work. As I rounded each curve, he swayed slightly, one raw red hand gripping the dashboard.

At the moment it seemed as if everything were about to gel irrevocably into a frozen silence, he ventured a comment, "Spring has come very early this year," and then lapsed again into autism, staring passively at the brilliant, glittering landscape rushing by, almost as if he were aware that his suffering both welded him to unstoppable outpourings of nature and at the same time forbid him any enjoyment of them. His metamorphosis toward death was, in other words, both invisible and metaphysically omnipresent. What my inkling of his mentality stirred in me is hard to describe, except to report that I was suddenly filled with a longing to become part of the exploding blossoms and chilly cascades of water reverberating on stone whose cathectic vitality released yearnings again for hyper-stimulation, recalling countless nights in which a glass stem streaming with plasticine smoke turned every cell of my body into pure process.

We were passing a café named le Relais, a word that implies refreshment, or renewal, an assumption that we are living in a reality riveted by relentless beginnings. So I pulled over. Would the Professor mind wasting a few moments for a drink? I asked timidly. We could sit on the terrace and talk about the research he wanted me to help him with.

He climbed painfully from the car with the boy's help, testily warning me, "You cannot trust their aperitifs here. Too much stem and leaf, not enough fruit." We were seated at an outdoor table under the sun, where I was sure that he would begin to discuss our project. Our small terrace was situated on a kind of esplanade cut into the slope of the mountain, near a torrent, and a harsh light pierced us from above, as if nailing our metal chairs to their shadows.

"That's the mountains for you," complained the Professor, "the sun shines and it's utterly scalding. You pass into the shade and the air cuts through you like a knife."

I brought up the subject of the research yet again, but the Professor interrupted me with rude insistence. "His insights," he said, referring to our writer, "have, lamentably, been all but forgotten! Nobody seems to recall that his most extravagant flights of inspiration...that they were the result of his dangerous liaisons with lowlifes! No one remembers that he broke his ties with the suffocating world of bourgeois literature."

Piped through the chasm of stone in which we were seated, his words pulverized my attention into anxiety. The more he veered from what I considered our main subject, the more perplexed, distressed and suspicious about the Professor's mental health I became. And yet I felt strangely identified with his careening words, which made me remember my crack-inspired hunger for underclass prostitutes.

Endlessly he spattered me with his staccato ramblings, his head darting about like a bird until his eyes fixed once again on the boy. The boy obviously could not understand a word of his French, but grinned back, brazen and glassy-eyed, until the Professor stopped speaking and devoured him with tragic, plaintive eyes.

"He's a local," said the Professor, flashing a knowing look at me that I could not interpret, while the boy bit at the dirty nail of one hand and peered at us from the edge of his glass of watered-down white wine. "In fact he's something of a casualty. As am I. You wouldn't know what they've done to both extremes of the social spectrum in this country, the aristocracy, which is, by the way, the class I come from, and traditional peasants like him and his family. All of us are becoming the victims of an ever fatter, more banal, middle class! Their very smugness makes me smell revenge in the air." And at this last sentence, perhaps because of its tone of bravado, the boy resolutely and noisily sucked the rest of the wine down.

Then the Professor asked me how comfortable I was with colloquial, nonliterary French, shifting once more abruptly into a wistful description of the boy's Alpine dialect, which resembled that spoken just over the border in Italy, on the other side of Mont Blanc, where most of the names ended in -az and where one could visit the city of Aosta, a word that is a corruption of Augustus, as in Caesar. I listened tensely, trying to deny to myself that his sudden swerves of context were symptoms of his mental deterioration, as my eyes anxiously swept past the other tables in an effort to avoid his darting gaze.

For the first time I noticed a woman sitting at a nearby table, her eyes cast to her feet, and I remembered that this was a mountain of more than one sanitarium. Her eyebrows had been drawn on her face and she was wearing a turban, perhaps to conceal a hairless cranium. Behind her was a red-faced old man wearing a wool cap, most likely an employee in a sanitarium, and further toward the edge of the esplanade was someone I had seen at our luncheon. He was very thin and about sixteen, also with the bald head of a chemotherapy patient. He was downing one of the several pastis overloading his table.

"They're from the sanitarium," said the Professor, catching my gaze with a kind of eerie satisfaction.

"You mean they let them drink?"

"It is very boring in the mountains," he snapped, and I thought I detected a note of contempt. The tone astonished me. I wondered if I truly knew what the professor's illness was and had the fleeting fear that it could be contagious. Suddenly I began insisting that we leave, that we had better go back up the peak before the afternoon meditation. With a shrug, the Professor pushed himself to an unsteady standing position and took my arm.

BY the time I had started the car, some of my disorientation had subsided. In an attempt to establish some context of conversation between myself and the Professor, I said, "They're rather severe up there at the sanitarium, aren't they? They run the place like a convent. Have you gotten to know any of the other...guests?"

"One woman who has a blood disease," the Professor replied flatly. Then he fell resolutely silent.

I sped onto the road a bit rudely, and the Professor was jerked forward; the frail raw hand was again extended to grasp the dashboard. The boy in the back seat tumbled sideways and let out a rude, boisterous laugh. The anxiety that had invaded me before returned and made me increase my speed. We passed one village after another at each small plateau, with cars parked around its single café.

"You must stop this driving," said the Professor suddenly. "It's making me ill." And indeed he did seem to have a certain pallor underneath the red, peeling skin. We sat in silence for several moments, when I ventured to say, "But it is getting late, isn't it? Perhaps we should be heading back up."

"No!" answered the Professor with fierce authority. And as he did, I noticed that the sky suddenly seemed to be getting darker. In fact, it would be night in another half hour. We sat there in tense silence while the darkness crept into the car. And as it did, I heard the breathing of the Professor deepen into relief. The boy began to hum a mindless tune to himself. Over and over its empty little intervals spilled into the darkness. And with each degree of darkness, the tune got slower and more deliberate.

THEN a flashlight pierced the trees. A fist rapped on the window next to the Professor's face. I bent over him to wind the window down, and a middle-aged man poked his head into the car.

"Has your car broken down?"

He was porcine and ruddy, and in the darkness, above his turtleneck, floated a fat neck and a falsely solicitous smile. I couldn't help thinking of the "ever fatter, more banal middle class" the Professor had grumbled about. "Have you had a breakdown?" he asked again.

The boy lunged and grabbed him by the head, managing to roll up the window to wedge it within the frame. The Professor sunk his teeth above the turtleneck. The man struggled and dug his neck against the window's edge, but the boy kept it jammed in place. Tremblingly the old man drank his fill, while the stranger's face changed from coagulated red to ashen gray.

The Professor fell back against the seat and smiled beatifically. His mouth was crimson and dripping. "So many things that were known have been forgotten, yet no one seems to care," he said as if explaining. His ancient face convulsed into a rictus of laughter, which shook his body with such force that I was afraid his ribs would snap. The effort had to have been too much for him, because it was cut off suddenly. His head fell to his chest and his body crumbled against the car door as if he were unconscious—or dead.

Blood trickled like rivers of liberty and appetite from the pallid neck attached to the unconscious head lodged in the window frame. The boy bent forward to take a drop of it onto the tip of his finger, brought it to his mouth, but stopped midway and sweetly extended it toward my face. His pointy tongue flicked back and forth seductively, from the wet hole of his gleaming mouth.

ANGEL BABY

MICHAEL THOMAS FORD

"**MAMA,**" said Willie Boy, "he's gone and done it again."

She looked up from her sewing to see her youngest son sitting in the middle of the room, the head of the orange and white cat in his hands. The rest of the cat's body lay on the floor next to him, blood puddled around the ragged hole in its neck.

"Angel Baby," she sighed, putting down the shirt she was mending and lifting herself wearily out of the chair. She walked over and took the head from the little boy. He cried as if she had taken away his favorite ball, reaching out his hands to her. Using the edge of her skirt, she wiped as much of the blood from his lips as she could, but still his face was smeared with rapidly drying streaks. As she scrubbed at his skin, he struggled against her, hitting her with his tiny fists.

"Angel Baby," she said firmly. "You all just sit still and let me clean you up some."

Angel Baby, unhappy, reluctantly allowed himself to be washed, although he whimpered from time to time when she scrubbed particularly hard. When she was satisfied that most of the blood was gone from his mouth, she picked up the cat's body and the head and went into the kitchen. Dropping the cat into a paper bag and folding the top over, she left it on the table while she went back to clean the blood from the floor. When she entered the room, she saw that Angel Baby had wiped his hands in the sticky liquid and was now happily licking it from his fingers and laughing.

"Lord Almighty, Willie, couldn't you watch him for even half a minute?" she said. "Now I hafta go and wash him all over again."

"Sorry, Mama," Willie Boy said quietly.

She picked Angel Baby up and took him into the kitchen. Filling the metal tub they used for bathing, she stripped off the bloody shirt and diaper and lowered the boy into it. He giggled happily as he splashed his hands in the water, turning it a pretty pale pink. As she washed him, she couldn't help but notice how nice the rosy color looked against the darkness of his skin, and she made a note to herself to make him a nightshirt that was the same color.

When Angel Baby was clean again, she dried him and put him down for a rest in his bed in the room with no windows. He settled down quickly. Unlike most small boys, he slept deeply and long, as though the unconscious was his natural habitat, and having to move about the world wide awake was a struggle he endured simply because she made him do so. As she stood over him, watching his tiny chest rise and fall, she found herself wishing that his father could be there to see him. Already she could see in Angel Baby's face the same hunger, the same desire to taste whatever pleasures were offered up to him, that had marked his father. But knowing as she did that wishing for what could never happen was just a waste of time, she closed the door quietly and went to wash the living room floor.

On Sunday morning she sat in the tight confines of the Holy Ghost Gospel Baptist Church and fanned herself with the program while the Reverend raged on about eternal damnation in a voice that shook the walls of her head. It was, she thought, far too hot to be talking about Hell. Even her thin cotton dress felt too close in the sweltering July heat, and she longed to loosen the bow at the throat. Instead, she nodded her head and shouted "Amen!" along with the rest of the congregation. Seated next to her, Willie Boy was restless in his Sunday trousers and stiff white shirt, and he kicked at the floor with the toe of his shoe. Once she pinched his leg to make him stop, but when he began again a few minutes later, she was too tired to even scold him. Instead, she sat with her eyes fixed on the Reverend and thought about how Angel Baby had smiled when she'd fed him that morning, his mouth turning up in a smile of pure joy, just as his father's had when last she'd seen him.

When the sermon was finally over, and the choir had sung its last "hallelujah," she stood and walked to the back of the church with Willie Boy in tow. They joined the long line of people waiting to say good day to the Reverend, and she smiled pleasantly at her friends and neighbors, who smiled in return. She had long ago stopped wondering what they said about her and her children behind their doors, since in her presence they were always kind and courteous. When she reached the door, she smiled brightly and shook the Reverend's hand.

"Thank you for the wonderful sermon, Reverend," she said, as she did every week. "It was, as always, very inspirational."

"Why, you're more than welcome," he answered. He put his hand on Willie Boy's head. "It's a pleasure to see you here, Willie." He looked back to Willie Boy's mother. "Angel Baby's almost four now, I guess. 'Bout time for his baptism, isn't it?" he said warmly.

She smiled back at him. "I guess it just about is, isn't it. I'll have to start thinking about that."

She took Willie Boy's hand in hers and squeezed it tightly as she made her way down the steps and through the crowd of people nodding to one another. She walked quickly down the road to the house, cutting across the cornfield, and didn't let go of Willie Boy's hand until they were well away from the Holy Ghost Gospel Baptist Church and the smiling man who wanted to push her Angel Baby under the water where he couldn't breathe. Again she thought about his father, and she had to close her eyes for a moment so that when she went inside Angel Baby wouldn't see her crying.

✳ ✳ ✳

WHEN Angel Baby was nearly five, and still safely unbaptized, he began to ask her about his father. "Who was he?" he said as she was putting him to sleep in the dark room.

"Who was who?" she asked, tucking the quilt about him and smoothing his pillow.

"My papa."

She paused. "Why do you ask me that?" she said.

"Willie Boy says my papa ain't the same as his."

She looked into his face. "Now don't you be listening to every word Willie Boy says, you hear. He don't know half as much as he think he does."

"He says the devil is my father," Angel Baby said. "That true?"

She laughed lightly. "Lord, no," she said. "He wasn't no devil. Wasn't no devil at all. Now go to sleep."

Kissing Angel Baby on the forehead, she shut the door. When she sat down to take up her sewing, her hands were shaking so she couldn't keep the needle still.

The first killing came several weeks later. It was earlier than she had expected, and she was annoyed to go into Angel Baby's room one morning to see him curled in a ball in his bed, blood smeared all over his new nightshirt. A trail of tiny red footprints led to the front door. He was breathing quietly and deeply, his mouth open in gentle wonder, and he looked so peaceful that she couldn't bring herself to wake him. Instead, she closed his door and washed away the footprints, humming as she scrubbed at the scarlet whorls made by his toes as he'd returned to his bed.

Later, she went to the store for some milk and learned that little Elsie Cooper had been the one. She'd been found in her bed by her mother, who woke the neighbors with her screams. "I always told her not to keep her window open at night," she'd cried as they had hurried her away from the sight of her daughter's bloodied throat. As she listened to the clerk recite the story, Willie Boy's mother couldn't help but remember what a stupid child the Cooper girl had been. Still, she felt for the mother. And when she approached the counter to pay for her purchase and several people looked at one another over her head, she pretended not to see them. "Lovely day, isn't it?" she said to the man who took her money.

There were more that summer, as the days grew longer and the nights were hot and filled with an unusual number of lightning storms. Old Cob Jones, found lying by his shack near the river with his dog howling beside him. The Samuels boy, the one not quite right in the head, who was always laughing at things no one else could see. Alice Peters, who they said went with any boy who asked her. As Willie Boy's mother washed her floor, she thought of how sometimes the Lord was just in His ways. And when some in town just happened to mention, as she passed by them on her way to church or to the store, that they hadn't seen such things for coming on nearly half-a-dozen years or so, she smiled at them from beneath her hat and walked more slowly.

Angel Baby and Willie Boy grew that summer as young boys will, both of them getting taller faster than she could let out the cuffs of their pants. To most eyes that saw them, they were brothers through and through, one nearing the age when he would move from boyhood to becoming a man, the other just beginning to come into his own self. But when she looked at her boys chasing one another through the fields, the bottoms of their feet pale and bare against the waves of dust they threw up, she knew that they would never really be brothers, not like most boys were.

As she watched their faces over evening supper, she thought also of that other long, hot summer of storms before Angel Baby was born. Willie Boy had been just about turning six. She was in love and spent the days washing clothes and baking in her kitchen, waiting for the hour when her husband would come home and kiss her again, his hands slipping up under her dress and making her laugh. She'd been happy then, she remembered, always singing, as though nothing in the world could change the way things were.

But one night, after a day in which the wind had blown dust through her house right after she'd swept and then she'd discovered the cream had soured in the pantry, he'd come home, bringing with him a tall, dark man whose powerful body fair near split open the seams of the overalls he wore. The man had reached out one big hand and shook hers, nearly breaking the bones of her fingers and smiling with teeth as white as fresh milk.

"This here's Big John," her husband said. "Guess as you can tell why that is. He's working with me down on the farm for the summer, and needs a place to stay. Guess it's okay if he stays here in the extra room."

The whole time her husband spoke, she'd been looking into Big John's eyes. Dark as the new moon, they seemed to her to have no ending to them, and she wondered if she looked long and hard enough if she'd see herself reflected in them the way the old cracked glass hanging over the sink sometimes surprised her by throwing her reflection back when she passed by.

"No," she said slowly, suddenly feeling very dirty and tired. "No, I don't suppose that would be a problem now at all."

Then they'd gone inside to dinner, and while the men sat and ate mightily of her cornbread and greens, she'd taken quick looks over at Big John, the muscles in his throat working slowly as he chewed her food and swallowed. For some reason, watching him eat what she'd made caused the little fingers of want to start working inside of her, and she'd sat with one hand in her lap as she ate, willing them to stop and praying her husband wouldn't see the betrayal in her face.

"That was mighty good," Big John had said when he was done. He looked at her and smiled. "Mighty good indeed."

Putting her hand over her mouth, she'd cleared the dishes as quickly as she could and brought him a piece of the warm peach pie she had cooling in the oven. At the last minute, she'd added a spoonful of the blackberries she'd been saving for Willie Boy's birthday, and when she cleared the plates away afterward, she took Big John's napkin stained with thick dark juice and held it to her lips.

Later that night, as Big John slept in the room next door and her husband hovered over her, pushing himself up into her, she imagined it was Big John between her legs, and she shook all over as she pulled her husband deeper into her and clawed at his back. The next day, after the men had left for work, she sent Willie Boy out into the yard to play while she went into the room where Big John had slept. Taking up the shirt he'd left slung over the back of the chair, she lay down on her bed and slipped her fingers inside of herself while she inhaled the smell of him and cried out his name.

Big John had been with them for two weeks when the killings started. Mostly it was men from the farm, found in the mornings with deep cuts on their throats, as though a razor had been drawn across them and all the blood let out into the thirsty ground. Sometimes it was boys, or men from town, but always they were the most handsome ones, the ones filled with great strength and promise, and their deaths left behind grieving wives and lovers.

"Sure like to know what's been doing them killings," she said as she dished out steaming, buttered peas at dinner. "Scares me to know someone's out there doing this."

Her husband had laughed. "Don't you worry none about that," he said. "Don't you worry none at all. Whoever t'is doing it, he's only got eyes for the menfolk."

He'd laughed again then, and that time Big John had laughed with him, his deep voice making her shiver and threatening to break through the walls. "No ma'am," he said as he picked up a chicken leg and bit into it. "Don't *you* have to worry none about it." Watching him tear the meat from the bones, she'd felt the wetness begin to slip onto her thighs.

* * *

THAT night she was awakened by the soft rustling of the quilt around her. She opened her eyes, and in the dark she saw Big John kneeling at the foot of the bed. He was naked, his body blacker even than the night around him. Her husband was between his legs, his mouth working up and down the length of Big John's hardness. Big John's hands were on her husband's head, urging him to move faster.

She watched wordlessly as her husband took Big John into his throat. There was neither shock nor fear in her. Something about the way they moved together made her unable to speak, as though she had caught a glimpse of two lovers through a bedroom window left open. They seemed to know each other well in this way, and she could only look on as the two men grunted and thrust against one another, the thick muscles of her husband's back glistening with sweat in the thin light from the moon as his head worked up and down the length of Big John.

The sight of the two men making love stirred her, and she found her hands moving under the quilt and between her thighs. She slipped her fingers inside herself and caught her breath as the pleasure began to work its way up her body. She moved with the two figures at the foot of the bed, her hand rocking in time with her husband's movements, as though through him she could also feel the hardness of Big John inside of her. As he increased his rhythm, she did also, her fingers tugging within her, urging her onward. One hand went to her nipple, which was thick with desire, and she worked at it silently, not allowing the moans within her throat to escape. Although she longed to reach out, to run her hands over the familiar curves of her husband's body and then onto Big John's unknown but dreamt-of one, to feel their heat and desire real and alive beneath her fingers, she felt that what they did now they did alone, with no thought of her.

She allowed herself to look up into Big John's face, and saw then that his eyes were fixed on hers, knowing that they had been for many minutes, watching her as she took pleasure in her own body. As she had the first time she saw him, she felt as though she were falling into the dark pools set into his head. He continued to stare at her as her husband brought him closer and closer, and she watched with interest as the muscles in his jaw and neck tensed as he grew near to releasing himself.

Then he did, his whole body arching back as he grabbed her husband's head and drove himself fully into the willing mouth. His eyes closed then, and his mouth opened in a roar both silent and deafening, as though his very soul were rushing out of his body and filling the room with its cry. She saw then his teeth—so oddly sharp, she was surprised she had never noticed before—and stained with something that glistened wetly against the whiteness. For a moment she stared into his open mouth, and then he opened his eyes and his lips came together once more.

Her husband turned to her, his eyes empty and wide. He crept toward her on the bed, and she saw that his mouth, too, was streaked both with darkness and with the pale remnants of Big John's seed. Still, when he knelt before her and looked into her eyes, she found herself wanting him, if only because he had so recently had Big John's hardness in his mouth. Pushing the quilt down, she spread her legs for him, watching as he moved his head between her thighs. She felt his mouth on her, his tongue working its way between her folds. She opened to him, taking him into her, and she knew that what had been held in his mouth was now inside of her. Her body began to shake, and she arched up into her husband, her fingers gripping the quilt as she smeared his face with her joy.

She looked over at Big John, who still knelt at the foot of the bed. Nodding to her, he slipped away into the darkness. Her husband rolled over and closed his eyes. Putting her hands on her belly, she slept, too, knowing that already inside of her a child was forming.

The next day when she woke, Big John was gone, his room empty of any sign that he had once inhabited it. Her husband could not look at her as he dressed, and spoke to no one as he worked the fields. That night, he was discovered wandering near the river, his clothes bloodied and his speech unintelligible. A short distance away, the body of a young man was found in the reeds, the throat ripped out and the head nearly severed. The people of the town, familiar as they were with the kind of justice necessary in such cases, found him guilty of the recent murders and hung him from the big oak near the church. She saw no need to mention Big John to them, and no one seemed to remember that he had recently been among them as they put the rope around her husband's neck. As she stood with Willie Boy in her arms, she had felt the child inside of her turn over as the women behind her whispered, "Poor woman. Hope her boy don't turn out crazy like his daddy."

* * *

ALMOST six years now, she often thought as she sat rocking near the fire or cutting the tomatoes for supper. *Almost six years since Big John went away.* Of her husband she thought almost nothing at all. Only when she looked at Willie Boy did she remember him, his features as he became a man so much like his daddy's. But even then it was as though she was looking at a faded photograph of a long-dead relative of whom she had only the vaguest recollection. After the hanging, it had been over, and no one spoke of it to her again. They knew it wasn't her fault. When she'd delivered Angel Baby on Easter Day, they had all wished her well and said, "He looks like his father."

It was in December, after the first heavy snowfall, that the last of the killings happened. They had continued all throughout the summer and fall, and although there was much talk in town, no one had ever been caught. Unconcerned by it, Willie Boy and Angel Baby had grown another two inches each and needed new clothes faster than she could make them. Then Charlie Potter was discovered in the shed behind his house, slumped over the woodblock where he'd been chopping kindling. She wasn't able to get to the blood in the snow, the blood that trailed in small drops across the field and up to her doorstep like a scattering of rose petals. Shortly after moonrise, there came a knock on the door. Drying her hands, she opened it and saw Calvert Briggs standing on her porch. He was wearing the same battered old hat he'd worn the day he'd come to her house nearly six years before.

"Well now, I guess you know what we're here for," he said, looking down at his boots. "I'm sorry to have to do it, but don't see as we have a choice. Guess we'd all hoped it died with the boy's father. Reckon you did, too. But maybe what he had in him just don't sleep. Maybe it just waits to the right time to wake up and start all over again."

She looked at the man's face. He glanced once at her face and then turned away. She looked past him at the crowd gathered in her front yard. They stood there silently, watching her. Her eyes briefly took in the blood in the snow, then the rope Able Gunner held in his gloved hands. She was thankful that it was winter, and that none of their big feet were crushing her flowers.

"I guess I knew it would come to this," she said. "Guess I always knew, even when I seen him hanging there. I prayed to God it wouldn't, but maybe some things even God can't stop."

Behind her, Willie Boy and Angel Baby were standing looking out at the man on their step.

"What's he want, Mama?" asked Willie Boy.

She put her hand on his head. "He's come on account of the killings," she said quietly.

She turned back to the man. "You all just make sure it's done right," she said. "I don't want him to suffer none. It ain't his fault."

The man nodded.

Thinking about Big John, she took her son by the hand, led him to the door, and gently pushed Willie Boy into the man's waiting arms. As the crowd closed around him, drowning out his cries of confusion, she shut the door. Gathering Angel Baby into her arms, she took him into the dark room. Sitting in the rocking chair, she hummed a little tune to drown out the rising noise from outside, and Angel Baby began to feed. *Just like his father*, she thought to herself as his tiny teeth parted her flesh, *and just as beautiful.*

THE WHOLE VAMPIRE THING

RON OLIVER

THE first sign that things were going to shit was when my agent called me.

He *called* me. As in, *he* picked up the telephone and *he* dialed it and *he* let it ring eight times until I dragged myself out of bed and answered it.

You see, Todd Benning had never let a telephone ring more than twice in his life. Of course, he had never *called* me more than twice in his life either, but that's a different story. At least it was, until that September morning in 1955.

"Paul, it's Todd Benning at the William Morris Agency."

He always announced himself like that, as if in the two or three days since we'd last spoken I had completely forgotten what he sounded like, who he was, and what agency represented me.

"Hello, Todd." I tried to open my eyes to look at the clock, but they weren't cooperating; I admitted defeat. "What time is it?"

"Late. Eight-thirty."

"In the morning?"

My attempt at humor was, as usual, greeted with a gale of laughter as realistic as his hairpiece and almost as comforting.

"That's funny. Listen, we gotta talk, pal."

More alarms went off in my head. *We gotta talk* was the worst thing you could hear. See, to an actor, good news is instant; you got the part, you got the check, the reviews are great. Bad news always takes more time; it's a gradual thing, like cancer.

And when the hell did he start calling me *pal?*

"Sure," I replied, dreading the next part of the conversation. "Shoot."

That's when the bottom fell out. The second worst possible thing he could have said to me. The end of the world as I knew it.

"Not over the phone," he said flatly. "Let's do lunch."

My bedroom turned to liquid and began spinning around me, and I felt sweat trickle down the inside of my armpits, instantly staining the ridiculously expensive satin sheets I wondered why I ever bought in the first place as the phone slipped from my grasp, hitting the hardwood floor of the apartment I was soon to lose for nonpayment of rent because I was surely about to be let go from the agency and would never work again in this or any business and would eventually be reduced to begging for quarters along Sunset Strip and sleeping in the bushes out behind the Chateau Marmont until the coyotes tore out my throat in my sleep and after they identified my mangled corpse through my dental records they'd bury me in an unmarked grave someplace in the Valley and the only mention my passing would merit would be a small piece in the back of *Variety* or *The Reporter* or, god forbid, *Dramalogue* and they'd still spell my name wrong and I'd simply disappear into oblivion forever....

"Great," I lied.

"Musso and Frank. Twelve thirty."

"I'll see you there—" I started to reply, but I was already talking to a dial tone.

I cleaned up fast and drove in from my place at the beach with the top down on my convertible T-Bird. Another of those famous L.A. traffic jams was blocking Sunset; a young actor named James Dean had just been killed in a car accident up the coast, and dozens of his fans were even now making their way to his last known address, a house nestled in the hills above the Strip. Carrying flowers, pictures, and candles, the faithful wept and mourned the passing of their idol. I felt a twinge of grief, not from the loss of a fellow actor—God knows if he was half as good as the studio wags were saying, I would've gladly taken a gun to him myself to get rid of the competition—but because I knew that if it'd been me smeared all over some rock on Highway 1, none of these people could've cared less.

The twinge passed as I cut down La Cienega and shot across Fountain to Hollywood. Nothing like a good shortcut to make your day, I always say.

Musso and Frank's Grill had been a venerable institution in Hollywood since the beginning of the century, and Joe, the pug-faced maitre d', had been with the place since it opened. As he led me through the dark oak room toward Todd's table, I tried to make small talk.

"So, Joe. How's business?"

"Business is business. Lunch is lunch. What do you want?"

Joe was like that. Warm and tender. He slapped the menu on the white linen tablecloth as I sat down across from my agent who, after acknowledging my arrival with a nod of his slicked head, continued talking on the table phone. I ordered a martini—we all ordered martinis back then—and leaned back into the thick leather of the booth to wait for Todd to finish his call.

"Look, Charlie, you know she can't act, I know she can't act. But you're making a movie about grasshoppers taking over the world, pal. Giant fucking grasshoppers. Jesus, you could put Ernie Borgnine in drag in your fucking movie and it wouldn't make a difference. Yeah, well, you read your contract, old boy, we gotta deal. She stays in or you pay in full to take her out. Yeah, you too Charlie. You, too."

He slammed the phone down and slugged back the tail end of his martini before he even looked at me.

"Fucking Charlie. Giant fucking grasshoppers. Jesus Christ. Joe!"

Todd touched his glass and Joe nodded from across the room.

"Crazy business," I ventured, anxious to steer the conversation toward the matters at hand.

"And the loonies are in charge," he smirked, suddenly looking at me. "How you feeling today, Paul?"

"Good. Great."

"Yeah?" He was still looking at me, the way you check under your shoe to see if you've stepped in any dog crap.

"Why?" I asked, getting suspicious.

"Nothing. You look kinda tired."

"Well, you woke me up early."

"Yeah. Early."

He kept staring at me as Joe brought another martini.

"Youse want food?"

"T-bone," Todd said quickly, not once in his life ever having looked at a menu. "Baked potato, extra sour cream. What's the vegetable today?"

"Cauliflower."

"I hate that shit. Just bring me an extra martini instead."

Joe looked at me, about to ask the same question, when Todd filled in the blank.

"He'll have a salad. No dressing. And water," he added, lifting my martini away from me and replacing it beside his own. Joe looked at me, shrugged and shuffled off to the kitchen.

"Jeez, Todd, I feel like we're on a date, you ordering for me and all."

He didn't laugh.

"Listen, Paul. We've got a problem."

I wished I had the martini back.

"Okay. A problem. We've had problems before—"

"Not like this. This one is...it's A list. You know that Siegel picture I had you up for?"

"Up for? No, you said I had it, Todd. *Had* it."

"Well, they took another look. Casting director over at Paramount saw you at that premiere Thursday night. He thought you were looking...well...frankly...he thought you were looking...old."

A knife pierced my heart. There are no words more feared in the vocabulary of Hollywood than that one.

Old. *Old.*

Todd drank the last of his second martini and started to reach for mine. I grabbed it back and finished it in one gulp.

The rest of the meal was a haze. As I chewed my flavorless lettuce, Todd talked about my future. Character work, he said. Cameo roles. Fathers. Elder statesmen. I'd still have a career, he assured me, but I'd never be a leading man again.

I drove home along Santa Monica Boulevard, feeling the sun on my face as I headed west. At first it felt good, comforting, soothing, an old friend in this time of dire need. And then I remembered something I'd heard on the radio about the sun and its effects on skin: drying, wrinkling. Aging.

I pulled over at Doheny, put the top up on the car, and drove the rest of the way home in the stifling darkness.

THE Center was nestled between two mountains, about half an hour's drive over roller-coaster roads inland from San Luis Obispo. At first glance, the place could've been a community college: low buildings, connected by tree-lined paths and framed by perfect blue sky above, deep green grass below. Only the high metal fence around the outside, humming with the promise of electric shock to any who dared climb it, hinted at the possibility that things were not what they seemed inside.

But I ignored that warning, as I must've ignored many others, and standing there in the front courtyard I took it all in—the sumptuous hills, the clean air, the occasional cry of a bird lost on its way toward the ocean. Real beauty, so far removed from the day-to-day artifice which was, and is, Hollywood. Yet in spite of the earthy majesty of it all, only one thought kept running through my mind.

This is my last resort.

In the weeks after Todd's pronouncement (*"Don't take it too badly. Everybody gets older, it's part of the business."*) I had launched into a flurry of activities: exercise classes, stretching techniques, vitamin supplements, ancient Chinese herbal packs, electric currents applied directly to the facial muscles. I drank my own urine, bathed in warm tomato juice, and even slept upside down for ten days; in short, anything that promised to reverse my downward slide into senior citizenship. But in spite of my efforts, the only change I noticed was the development of severe migraines, brought on no doubt by a continuous rush of blood to the head during my nocturnal suspensions, and severe halitosis. You try drinking your own piss for two weeks and see what it does to your breath.

It was when things were looking the most hopeless, and I had resigned myself to a life of playing Big Daddy in off-off-off Broadway productions of *Cat on a Hot Tin Roof*, that the note appeared in my mailbox. A thick cream envelope, embossed with a gothic "C" on the back; there was no return address, just my name written in clean black script on the front. My first thought was: *A party! What color can I wear to hide the fact that senility is just around the corner?* But upon opening the envelope I discovered something quite different; an invitation, to be sure, but not to a social event.

Dear Mr. Douglas, the handwritten letter began. *Your name has been forwarded to us by a friend who feels you could benefit from our services. We at The Center invite you to contact us by phone or mail for a further consultation regarding our exclusive therapy guaranteed to slow and, in many cases, stop entirely…*

My eyes raced ahead to complete the sentence and my breath caught in my throat as I read—

…the process of aging.

I clenched the letter and read the last word again.

Aging.

I was packed and on the road by noon.

THE Motherlode Bar was jammed to its beer-soaked rafters on the Sunday afternoon when I met Carl. It was the middle of December 1976, as close to winter as we get in Southern California, and he was wearing white jeans. White, three months after Labor Day, in a gay bar in Los Angeles. I decided any man brave enough to do that deserved a beer, possibly an import, and sidled up to him with a fresh Heineken in my hand.

"Beer?" I offered him the bottle.

"Yeah, it is," he countered.

"Do you want a beer?" I persevered. He looked me over; my muscles were taut and lean, my features precise and unwrinkled, my shining black hair thick and full. In the past two weeks I'd had over twelve auditions, with call-backs on half of them and a definite "yes" on two. He cocked his head and gave me the sideways glance I would eventually come to know as his "what the fuck" look.

"What the fuck," he muttered, taking the beer. He looked at my now-empty hands. "Where's yours?"

"I don't drink," I replied, which was more or less the truth. After being on The Center's diet program for over twenty years, avoiding alcohol had become second nature to me.

Carl shrugged and toasted my invisible glass. As he chugged the beer back I watched the muscles in his throat work; solid and sinewy, they undulated like a cobra beneath his copper skin and hinted at the chiseled physique beneath his tight black T-shirt and the aforementioned unfashionable jeans. As he finished the drink, he leveled me with his dark Asian eyes.

"What's your name?"

"Paul. Paul Douglas."

"You look familiar. You hang out here often?"

"Not really."

"Well, you look familiar."

I shrugged, feigning nonchalance.

"I work on television."

He looked at me blankly.

"Like, fix them?"

"No," I replied, probably slightly more haughty than I meant to be. "I'm on TV. 'Upstairs with Ed'? I play Ed."

Carl nodded and his gaze drifted down just below my belt buckle.

"I don't watch TV," he said, putting the beer back to his mouth and drinking deeply, never once taking his eyes off my crotch.

I don't *watch* TV.

The sentence followed me out to the parking lot and stayed in my head long after I finished fucking Carl in the backseat of my T-Bird.

DR. Carrington, my case physician, had already explained most of The Center's procedure to me but there was simply no way to prepare myself for how *jarring* it felt to be strapped naked to an operating table.

I had opted for Plan A, euphemistically referred to as "Eternal Youth." I was measured, weighed, and had every possible test known to man performed on any and all veins, organs, and orifices in my body before I was "cleared" for the operation. But no matter how many times Carrington told me, I still couldn't quite figure out what exactly was going on.

The operating room was unlike one I had ever seen before, either in real life or on a movie set. First of all, it was enormous, with high, dark walls and a stainless steel floor dotted with drainage grates. Then there were the nurses; far from being the delicate flowers one normally associates with the Florence Nightingale set, these women looked like they'd been recruited from the Soviet wrestling team, and I'm sure they handled me with the same care they'd give to a wily opponent.

However, the strangest part of the entire affair, the thing I found the most unnerving, was the significant lack of operating instruments of any kind. Not a scalpel nor a pair of scissors to be found anywhere. Just me, naked, bound with leather belts to a low-rising gurney, positioned with painstaking attention to detail by Olga and Inga in what seemed to be the exact center of the room. I was about to question the whole situation when Dr. Carrington entered. He was in his late forties, with thinning hair and spectacles, and he reminded me very much of the kind of man you saw in those Driver's Ed films at high school: *Red Asphalt, Speeding Death, The Last Date*...that sort of thing.

"Well...are we all ready then?"

I nodded. Well, at least I tried to nod; it was a bit tricky what with the tight metal band around my head and the rubber ball gag in my mouth.

"Mffgh gghhhff?" I asked.

"Of course you are. Everything's going to work out just fine. All of our tests showed you're the perfect candidate for this procedure. Now I just want you to lay back and relax...."

At which point he produced one of the largest hypodermic needles I have ever seen.

He shot a stream of the glistening yellow syrup up into the air and, satisfied there were no air bubbles, lowered it to my arm. I felt the needle's point press against my vein and then puncture it with the dullest of pops, and the silver itch of metal sliding deep into my flesh. I looked up into the harsh overhead lights of the room and the silhouetted head of Dr. Carrington, nodding as he depressed the plunger.

"You're going to be just fine...."

The lights brightened and everything went white.

IN my dream, it's always 1943.

I'm sixteen years old and home from school early. My mom is at work at the munitions plant, my dad is seeing active combat and, although I don't know it at the time, he's two weeks away from having his legs blown off somewhere in the Aleutian Islands. I'm sitting alone at the kitchen table in our old house in Sacramento, eating Frosted Flakes from the box and listening to "Inner Sanctum" on the radio. The Chicken Heart That Ate Cleveland is working its way up Baldwin Avenue and even though I know it's just a dumb radio show, and that Arch Oboler, the guy who writes it, is probably some old drunk, I'm still caught up in the sound of the chicken heart;

ba-thump...ba-thump...ba-thump...

I look through the french doors in the kitchen, out to the backyard, where Joey Ferrara is mowing the lawn.

...ba-thump...ba-thump...ba-thump...

Although he's just turned nineteen, and built like a prizefighter, they say he failed his medical exam and won't be going off to war with the rest. It's caused his family a considerable amount of shame, especially since there are rumors going around the neighborhood that there's nothing *physically* wrong with Joey. They say he flunked the mental tests, and some folks even say something about him being perverted. I remember overhearing my mother whisper to my Aunt Ellen, "Joey has unnatural cravings..."

And I wonder just how unnatural they might be.

...ba-thump...ba-thump...ba-thump...

Suddenly, Joey is standing in the kitchen, his shirt off and dangling from his back pocket. His dark hair hangs in his eyes, his smooth chest glistens, and he opens his full red lips revealing a perfect line of teeth the color of the pearl handle on my favorite penknife and says, "Do you mind if I have a drink?"

...ba-thump...ba-thump...ba-thump...

I move to the sink like I'm walking in quicksand and as I pour him a glass of water I can feel his breath on the back of my neck and I turn around with the glass half filled and he's naked in front of me, every muscle in his body taut and straining, skin bronzed to a scarlet except for where he usually wears his shorts which is ivory white and perfectly framing his thick, long cock, throbbing, pulsing with a life of its own.

...ba-thump...ba-thump...ba-thump...

The glass shatters when it hits the floor and Joey pulls me toward him, somehow undressing me with three quick strokes of his arms. I can feel his heat, the iron poker between us, as he licks my chest, my nipples hardening to stone at his touch. He pushes me down onto the kitchen table and my arm hits Tony the Tiger, sending hundreds of crunchy, tasty, sugar-frosted flakes of corn scattering across the floor. I try to move, to touch him, to run my hand along the rock solid waves of his abdomen but the leather straps hold me firmly in place and suddenly the kitchen darkens and becomes the operating room, the walls stretching up into the infinity of The Center, and Joey Ferrara is ten feet tall and his gigantic dick is two feet long and it hisses and snaps like a cobra, arching blindly in search of its victim.

...ba-thump...

Joey's brown eyes turn white, blinding white, scorching me as his rough hands force my legs apart and shove my knees to my chest, exposing the red pucker of my ass to the suddenly cold air.

...ba-thump...

My head slides off the edge of the table, lolling at the end of my neck, and the world is upside down and I see a little yellow sundress on a thin, waif-like woman with cruelly short hair and big eyes and I remember her from a movie I won't see for another twenty years as she says

this is no dream! This is really happening!

and I force my head back up to look at Joey, whose eyes are still burning brightly, his long, tanned torso gleaming, and his monstrous phallus swollen and pounding—

...ba-thump...

—the slit at the end gaping like a mouth and dear god oh jesus oh jesus there are teeth oh god there are sharp white teeth in the mouth dear god oh jesus

—*his cock has teeth*—

It plunges up into my ass and I feel it biting me, biting my bowels and further up into my belly, the heat, burning, hot knives...

RINGGGGG. Ring*ggg*...

I woke up in 1956 and rolled over, reaching across Ken, a blond AWOL marine who had been looking for a place to crash and fifty bucks on the side, and fumbled the phone from its cradle.

"Yeah?"

"Paul. It's Todd Benning, at the William Morris Agency."

"Yeah, hi Todd..."

"They want you, pal."

I sat up. The marine didn't move.

"What?"

"You heard me. You gotta be at MGM for costume fitting today at three. Nick fucking Ray himself said you were the best of the bunch. And get this...he thought you might've even been too young, but he's gonna take the chance," Todd chuckled.

My reflection in the mirror above the bed showed me a man with rippling muscles, shining hair and a taut and handsome face glowing with youth and vigor. But the image of what I had become no longer startled me as it had in the first few weeks after the procedure. In fact, I had gotten quite used to looking twenty-five years old again.

"Too young!" Todd repeated, still laughing. "What the hell are you doing to yourself these days, pal?"

I glanced down at Ken, his pale skin almost blue in the diffused light of my bedroom, his green eyes staring lifelessly up at the ceiling. What little blood of his I didn't drink had dried on the ragged tendons and torn flesh at his throat and I was relieved to see that not a drop had stained my expensive sheets. I picked up the fifty dollar bill I'd left for him on the night table and tucked it back into my wallet. On one hand, he wouldn't be needing it anymore; on the other hand, he wouldn't get court-martialed either.

"Clean living, pal," I lied to my agent. "Just good, clean living."

ALL considered, I took to the whole vampire thing surprising well.

I'd spent four months at The Center after my procedure, taking therapy classes and learning how to live my new life: the correct way to insert the leaded glass contact lenses; how to apply the dense sun block which would allow me to venture outside during daylight hours; how to measure and mix the freeze-dried plasma product necessary for my new diet. It was, as Dr. Carrington explained, a brave new world for me to discover and, ultimately, conquer. I was just happy to see the wrinkles disappear from around my eyes.

Of course, there were some problems with The Center's program; after all, nothing is perfect. And on occasion, the convenient envelopes of plasma flakes ("*add water, stir, and drink*") were either unavailable or, more frequently, unsatisfying. In situations like that, Carrington had what he referred to as a Contingency Plan, an option for emergency use only.

I will admit the killing was difficult at first.

Not the morality of it, of course. I was, after all, an actor in Los Angeles; given the huge dose of crap the town serves up daily, murder had crossed my mind more than once. And while civilization has certainly done its part to pave over our more basic instincts, they're still there, humming beneath our consciousness like live wires, dangerous if exposed. The instinct to hunt, the instinct to kill, the instinct to survive—they're all intact. The only thing we have to do is relearn them.

I'm proud to say I was an apt pupil.

We hunted at The Center, in the wide open fields, the valleys, the mountains. Sometimes they were runaways, scruffy, apple-faced mid-westerners picked up at the bus station with the promise of a screen test; kids weren't as cynical in the fifties and the old twin lures of fame and fortune worked every time. Occasionally they were working actors or actresses, in between jobs and looking for their next gig. They were told it was live theater of a sort, but they certainly couldn't have expected to be stripped naked and running for their lives from a pack of human jackals, intent on tearing open their bodies to savor the warm, musky meat inside. I remember taking down a kill on the side of a mountain, a handsome kid of about twenty whose genitals I tore away with one bloody swipe, when through his uncomprehending terror a sudden recognition dawned: "You...you're the guy on that toothpaste commercial...?" he drawled in a soft Texas twang.

I smiled, his blood slickly smeared across my mouth, and nodded.

"Yes. Yes I am."

"Wow..." he sighed, thick red juice spurting from the gouge in his groin. "I gotta tell my mom I met somebody famous...."

His eyelids fluttered and his head slumped back on the grass. I sat there a moment, letting the silence of the night envelope us both, and considered my future.

I had become a murderer. I needed human blood to stay young. I was morally perverse, pathologically violent, and unquestionably evil.

I was going to be a star.

IT'S funny about Carl.

I'd had every intention of making him a one-night stand; a quick fuck, slash of the throat, drain his blood, toss him in the ocean. The usual. But to my surprise, while sex with him was quite good, the conversation afterward had been even better; in spite of his perfect body and flawless face, his most stimulating organ turned out to be his mind. For although I appeared to be no more than in my mid-twenties, in fact I was actually well past middle age and my physical contemporaries were beginning to bore me, the dramas and neuroses of their sweet young lives were things I'd long since experienced and forgotten. What clubs were hot or cold, what drugs were in or out, whose haircut cost more and where he got the money—these were the issues of the day to young Hollywood, and they held no interest for me.

Carl didn't seem to care about any of these things either. He was an artist, "a painter of no particular reputation," as he put it. He'd had a few showings around town, and the galleries knew his work, but aside from the occasional sale to elderly gay men who wanted to spend an afternoon admiring his ass while he hung the painting, he hadn't achieved the kind of notoriety he said claimed to disdain but which, I found out later, he secretly desired.

He was, he said, an "old soul" and he'd unfailingly accepted many things about me that might have given younger souls pause: the skin cream I couldn't step out of the house without first applying; the stench of the "protein flakes," as I called them, that I blended and drank every dawn before uttering so much as a "good morning" to him; the infrequent "visits" to the darker parts of town when the protein ran out.

While I knew he had accepted it all, I didn't really grasp the depth of his understanding until late one afternoon, about six months after we'd met. We'd stopped along the edge of the Malibu bluffs to watch the sunset. There was a long moment of silence, the kind you have with someone you know well, and I could sense the question coming before it left his lips.

"Do you love me?" he asked flatly.

"Yes," I replied, startled by the abruptness of my answer. "Yes, I do."
He looked to the ocean, the golden light fading on his face.
"You have secrets even I don't know about."
It wasn't a question. It was a statement.
He didn't wait for my response. He took my hand in his and held it very, very tightly.
"If you ever jump," he said without a smile, "I'm going with you."
The sun dropped off the edge of the earth and darkness rolled in like fog.

I LET Todd Benning go in the fall of 1969.

Things had been reaching a boiling point for some time, but I guess it was the incident in the house on the hill that really set it off. After my dramatic physical change in 1956, work poured in; everybody wants an actor with experience and youth, and I had both in spades. The Nicholas Ray picture did some money, and for a brief time I was being touted as the next James Dean. But that stopped when the *original* James Dean became the next James Dean; it seemed that not only vampires live forever.

I worked in dozens of films through the sixties, some memorable, some, to quote Leonard Maltin, quite forgettable. In retrospect, I probably should've chosen better projects, but at the time I was just so thrilled with the idea of working constantly, I took anything that was offered to me: kitchen-sink dramas, lame comedies, a few unthrilling thrillers.

And then along came the job that killed my career in feature films for good.

You've probably heard about it, you might have even seen it on video or that late night turkeyfest on Channel 8. If not, let me just say this: *Daniel Boone 2000* wasn't supposed to be a bad movie. In fact, the original script was an exciting science fiction adventure, full of great special effects and breathtaking action. But the studio had a change of management in 1965 and in order to cut costs, we ended up shooting in Italy. The crew, none of whom spoke English, hated the director; the director, who couldn't speak a word of Italian, hated me, and I, unable to translate between the two languages fast enough, ended up hating my life.

When it was finally released, more than three years later, audiences stayed away in droves. The reviews were unanimous: "Possibly the worst movie ever made!" (L.A. *Times*); "Not bad enough to be great, not good enough to be awful!" (*Washington Post*); and a personal favorite, "Paul Douglas stinks up the screen" (*Variety*").

Overnight, my stock in Hollywood dropped like a dead gull. My asking price plummeted, my credit dropped from above the title to somewhere before "Catering By," and my telephone simply stopped ringing.

So I decided to do what any movie star would do when his career hit the skids.

I went to TV.

None of this, however, is an excuse for what happened that night on the hill. It just...happened.

RINGGG...ringg....

"This is Todd Benning."

It was after midnight and Todd was still at work; there were advantages to having a manic depressive for an agent.

"Todd. It's me. Paul."

"Oh. Paul. Right. Listen, sorry I didn't call you back today—"

"It doesn't matter, just listen—"

"Hang on—"

"No, Todd, listen—"

"Just let me get your file—"

"Fuck the file, Todd! I need your help!!"

Silence for a moment. When he spoke again, Todd's voice was quieter, almost human.

"What kind of help? You mean like money?"

"I need you to come and get me. Come and get me, Todd. Right now."

In less than thirty minutes, Todd Benning was throwing up.

He had come into the house on the hill through the open front door.

"Paul? Are you in here?"

But he stopped dead in his tracks when he saw the blood on the carpet and the five corpses scattered across the living room floor. I struggled to my feet in the middle of it all, dazed, naked and covered in glistening red gore, and held out my hands as if to show him what had happened.

"I didn't mean to kill them all," I slurred, but by then Paul had collapsed to his knees, already throwing up all over his seven-hundred-dollar suit.

It was the truth. I'd met the handsome young man who was my intended victim at a Silverlake club; he'd seemed slightly out of place and a little disoriented, but he had a winning smile and a pronounced bulge showing through his faded jeans; good enough for me. After a quick hand job in the toilet to get him in the mood, we drove up to his hillside home off Cañon Drive. In the middle of his living room with its immaculate white carpet and perfectly matched white sofa and chairs, we undressed for each other. I saw he was slighter than I usually liked, his ribs visible through his well-tanned flesh. But he had the clearest blue eyes I'd ever seen, almost shining in the darkness, and an outstanding cock which, as he slid his Lee jeans down to his ankles, sprung out toward me long and narrow, with a pronounced curve to the left.

It had slid easily down my throat and, to my delight, he was agile enough to reposition himself so his ass could act as a willing host to my stiff prick. We rocked gently at first, his thrusts matching my own, until the fire began to build in both of our bodies and we picked up the pace. I felt the flared head of his member swelling in my gorge, pulsing as he readied himself.

"I'm gonna come—" he grunted, and his salty heat hit the back of my throat in a torrent as I bit down hard on the base of his dick.

He shrieked in horrified pain and lurched back away from me, his cock dangling from the torn ligaments at his crotch. He tried to form words, but couldn't stop screaming—

...ba-thump...

...ba-thump...

...ba-thump...

It should've ended quickly, but when I stood to finish the kill I was suddenly overcome with a intense feeling of vertigo. I staggered, swaying on my feet, and tumbled onto the couch. The room spun and whirled around me and when I looked at a lamp, I saw nothing but the brightest and most brilliant colors streaming out from the golden bulb. Flowers seemed to spring from the walls and the carpet became a sea of beautiful blue water, waves lapping at my ankles as I floated on my couch boat. As I realized what was happening, I glanced over at the young man and his screams became opera, a beautiful aria he sang at the top of his lungs, his accompaniment the fountain of blood in his lap.

That was my first and last experience with LSD.

Suddenly, the door burst open and people came into the house, among them, a beautiful blonde woman I recognized from a movie I'd seen earlier that week about Young Hollywood Starlets. They began screaming, reeling in terror at the scene before them, and from deep inside of me, through the shimmering waves of the drug I had ingested via the young man's blood, a cold wave of instinct rose up.

They had to die.

It was a bloodbath. The acid in my veins, combined with the killing skills I had developed over the years, gave me strength I had never felt before. Without a single pause, I tore those Beverly Hills socialites from limb to limb, gouging out their eyes, slashing their fine throats, ripping at their ivory skin until nothing but lifeless sacks of meat and blood remained. And when it was over, when that pristine white room looked like an abattoir, I fell onto my prey and I drank....

One of the advantages to being with a big agency like William Morris is that when things go wrong, even horribly wrong, they can usually get you out of trouble with just a few phone calls. In this case, it involved pulling in some favors at LAPD homicide—apparently someone quite high up had a daughter who needed an agent—and then framing a wandering group of stoned hippies for the crime. A Beatles fan at the office suggested writing *Helter Skelter* in blood over the couch, a stroke of brilliance for which he was rewarded with a promotion to VP, and the crime became legendary around the world. You may never have heard of Sharon Tate or any of my other victims, but everybody knows who Charlie Manson is.

Anyway, my name was kept out of the papers, and my ass off the electric chair, so needless to say I was happy with the outcome. But not so my agent. Todd had been on sick leave since the night of the killings, and hadn't answered any of my phone calls, so I decided to pay him a visit to check up on his health. It took some convincing and a broken finger to get him into the car, but he stopped fighting me by the time we reached the bluffs atop Mulholland Drive, high above the city.

"Nice night."

Todd looked pale under his tan and despite his expensive leather jacket, he was shivering.

"Paul, look, I don't know what you think you're doing—"

I took him firmly by the arm and pulled him out of the car, toward the embankment.

"You've been a good agent, Todd. Really. The best. But I think, given everything that's happened lately, it's time we parted company."

He gaped in terror down into the darkness of Coldwater Canyon, hundreds of feet below.

"No...Paul...I told you...I told them at work...I won't say anything...ever...I swear. I swear."

That made me laugh.

"I'm supposed to trust an agent?"

"I'm a team player, Paul. I would never do anything to hurt you. Or William Morris."

I considered this; he was definitely a company man, loyal to a fault. Maybe he was telling the truth....

On the other hand, he might change agencies.

"Sorry, Todd."

As I mentioned before, 1969 was the year I let my agent go. He fell easily a hundred and fifty feet, straight down into the backyard of the Vice President of Development at CBS, and landed in an empty swimming pool. His neck snapped instantly.

When they performed the autopsy, they discovered nothing unusual other than the fact that a seemingly perfectly happy executive at one of the biggest agencies in the country had committed suicide for no apparent reason. I mention this because I want to make it clear that Todd Benning had all of his own blood when he hit the ground. I didn't suck a drop out of him.

Professional courtesy, you know.

"UPSTAIRS with Ed" finished its seven year run on ABC in 1979, and a spin-off called "Off the Top" was developed for my character. You probably remember it, the wacky misadventures of a young, good-looking guy, played by yours truly, whose dead uncle leaves him a barber shop which he must run successfully for one year in order to collect the rest of his inheritance—one million dollars. The show was an instant hit and the money was rolling in; I was back on top again. I had a team of agents now, none of whom I got to know well enough to risk revealing my secret. They worked hard for me anyway; I never waited in line, had the best table at every restaurant in town, and my whims and needs were catered to by network flunkies and studio executives alike.

But my celebrity had a price; Carl and I could never been seen together. While the Holy Trinity of Andy, Halston, and Bianca may have made homosexuality chic in New York, it was still a long way from Studio 54 to Peoria, and nobody was going to watch a sitcom starring a faggot. Everything was orchestrated: premieres, parties, even days at the beach were entirely organized by the studio or the network, with my handlers always making sure I had an attractive woman on my arm or two more in the car.

Somehow Carl survived all of this, a shadowy figure in the corner of the room, a part of my life but unable to share it. I suppose the worst was seeing him alone up in the balcony during the Emmys while I sat front row and collected two trophies in one night. Standing onstage next to an ex-hooker who had become the star of her own prime-time cop show, I could thank my agents, my manager, my accountant, my parents, but not the one man who deserved it most. When I caught his eye later at the party, he just cocked his head and gave me that look

—*what the fuck*—

Yet in spite of the pressures, we managed to find time together, alone. With my baseball cap pulled down tight and dark glasses hiding my eyes, Carl and I could spend whole days wandering through the hills, visiting crass tourist attractions, eating cheap Mexican food which I couldn't actually digest but would wolf down as if ravenous. Then, after a quick visit to the toilet to "freshen up" and a few minutes of frenzied vomiting to get the foul-tasting charred flesh out of my gut, I'd be good as new.

But I never told him the truth.

Logically, you might wonder how this was possible. How could I conceal from my lover the unusual behavior, the odd hours, the frequent return from strange parts of town with the smell of another man's body upon me?

Two words: The Seventies.

The end of that decade was unlike anything the gay world had ever seen. Drugs were everywhere, booze was cheap, and the mindless rhythms of disco fueled the flames of passion like gasoline. Half-naked men sweated their way from Silverlake to West Hollywood without once missing a beat and it seemed the party would go on forever. And if, in the middle of all this, the occasional leatherboy or gym kid would suddenly disappear, never to be seen again, it was just assumed that the fun had worn off for him and he had gone back to Indiana or Iowa or wherever the hell he had come from in the first place.

Of course, I was very careful to follow Dr. Carrington's protocol, burning their bodies and dumping the ashes into the ocean north of Zuma, where not even the hardiest surfer could find them.

I had learned my lessons well.

To start the eighties off right, I bought a new house in Malibu

Colony, balanced delicately on the side of a hill with a magnificent view of the ocean. There was a glass-walled living room, enough bedrooms and bathrooms for a visiting soccer team, and an unfinished basement which I had soundproofed and equipped with a heavy steel door. This was my private space, I explained to Carl; an inner sanctum where I could unwind entirely alone. It was to be off limits to everyone, even him, and while this caused a six-day fight between us, he still moved into the house in time to find out who shot J. R. on the season premiere of "Dallas." It was on opposite the season premiere of "Off the Top" and demolished us in the Nielsens, but I didn't particularly care; Carl was back.

That Christmas, our first in the new house, I gave him a Ferrari. He gave me a Golden Retriever puppy we named Tom, after the Tom of Finland print the dog knocked off the wall and peed on during its first night in the house.

Eternity looked good from there.

I FOUND Carl's ring in the sand three days after the earthquake of '94.

Tom was nearly fourteen, ancient in retriever years. I was walking him on the beach, revisiting his favorite dunes and shrubs, when I saw something glint down near the water. At first I thought it might have been some change, maybe a quarter lost by an anxious, ice cream-seeking child from one of the houses further up the shoreline. But on closer examination, it was the gold ring I'd given him when he went into the hospital. I read the inscription aloud, the wind carrying my words out to sea.

I don't watch TV is what it said.

He'd laughed the first time he read it, laughed until he coughed, choking on the tube down his throat. A nurse had hurried into the room, clearly expecting at least an emergency, or possibly a soon-to-be-available bed. When she saw Carl grinning around what he referred to as his "mouth plumbing," she glared at me.

"Mr. Douglas, visiting hours are over."

I kissed him gently on the cheek, tasting the flat chalkiness of the makeup he wore to cover the lesions, and slid the ring onto the third finger of his left hand.

"You are my knight in shining armor," I whispered so the nurse wouldn't hear.

He couldn't speak, so he squeezed my hand in reply and nodded, his eyes moist. I tossed the nurse a wink as I moved to the door.

"You ever sneak in here and jerk him off while he sleeps?"

She looked suitably aghast.

"Certainly not!"

I feigned surprise.

"Well you should. He loves that."

She sputtered something, and I gave Carl one last grin before I stepped into the hall and broke down in tears.

They called it GRID at first, Gay Related Immune Deficiency, but a rose by any other name is still poisonous and no matter what clever label they attached, my love, my life, was dying. I won't bore you with the details; it's a depressingly familiar story. I had begun to notice a change in the taste of some of my kills around 1982, but simply put it down to an iron deficiency. However when the news surfaced, slowly, deceptively, about a fatal disease attacking homosexuals, I immediately began stockpiling plasma flakes and curtailing my forays into the city for fresh blood.

Carl became sick right away. Exhaustion first, followed by frequent nausea and then chronic fatigue; I often found him asleep at his easel, passed out with the wet paintbrush still in his hand. My studio health plan didn't cover him, even though we had been living together for half a decade, and he didn't have any insurance of his own, so I paid for his care myself by cashing in on some investments and eventually mortgaging the house.

"Off the Top" never really recuperated from the ratings bashing it took opposite "Dallas" and within six months it was canceled. For the first time in almost thirty years I was without work. My agents huddled, promising they were trying to find "the right project" for me, a polite way of saying I was old news. I hadn't aged, but my name had, and although I could still compete with the younger actors in the looks department, I was a too-familiar face on the nation's TV screens.

In Hollywood, as everywhere, familiarity breeds contempt and I was in the middle of mating season.

But Carl needed medication and weekly visits to a doctor who seemed to charge by the millisecond, so I took whatever work I could get. I did guest shots on elephant graveyards like "Fantasy Island" and "Love Boat"; celebrity quiz shows, where half-drunk has-beens competed for absurd prizes which they invariably sold to prop up the scale paycheck they received for their appearance. I even did a car show, signing autographs and posing for pictures next to the other remaining cast members of "Upstairs with Ed," all of whom were stunned to see me looking so young.

Elizabeth, whom you'll remember as Tanya Lee, the reformed hooker on the show, spent most of the week trying to find the plastic surgery scars behind my ears.

"It's fabulous, you can't see a thing!" she exclaimed through lips tightened to a grimace by her own botched nip and tuck. "Fabulous!"

I just nodded and smiled with my arm around Cher, a senior citizen from Kansas, who smelled like peanut butter and kept telling me I was the most important man in her life.

My kills during this time were confined mostly to South Central Los Angeles; the sudden rise in gang violence during the eighties gave me perfect cover. For every ten murders attributed to the Bloods or the Crips or any of the other factions in the neighborhood, I could claim at least two undetected. While their blood was often tainted with the cursed virus that ravaged Carl, it didn't seem to have any adverse effect on me with the exception of a sinus headache which passed quickly. The only danger was the occasional crack addict in the mix, but they were easy to spot, shambling zombies lurking in the shadows, venturing out only long enough to satisfy their craving. They tended to give me a wide berth anyway, probably sensing a kindred spirit in their midst.

Hunting was easy in this war zone, but my heart wasn't in it. Most nights I simply took one down, finished him off and returned to the house in time to walk Tom who, by now, had grown into the size of a small moose. Later, curled up together in bed, I would read to Carl whose tastes had become wildly eclectic since his illness; Proust one week, followed by V.C. Andrews and then The National Enquirer if the spirit moved him.

He had been released from the hospital after a month-long stay; they called it "outpatient treatment" but he knew as well as I did that they'd sent him home to die. Still, we kept our spirits up, tossing hope back and forth between us like a balloon, afraid to let it touch anything for fear it would break. Our long walks on the beach became shorter and shorter, until one day he couldn't leave the house anymore. I moved a bed into his studio so he could paint when he wanted to, sleep when he needed to, and always see the ocean for inspiration.

It was raining the first time Carl died.

We'd stayed in all day, watching Whatever Happened to Baby Jane on AMC, which we had agreed didn't count as actual TV, and reciting the dialogue to each other

—Butcha are, Blanche! Y'ayr in the chair!—

and while we were sitting within a few feet of the roaring fireplace, Carl shivered constantly under his sweaters and blankets, his teeth chattering in spasms. The movie had ended and I was in the kitchen getting his four o'clock medication when Tom begin howling. I called into the living room—

"Honey, pet him or something, he's lonely."

There was no answer and Tom kept howling.

"Honey? Carl?"

I dropped the pills and they scattered across the floor like those goddamned Frosted Flakes in my dream as I ran out of the room.

"Carl?"

He was on the floor, shivering violently, his frail body trapped in the heavy blankets. His eyes were bright with terror as he struggled to sit up and I hurried to his side to help. I pulled him onto my lap and held him, held his beautiful head in my arms, cradling him, rocking him, and whispering stupid, impotent words as my lover, my Carl, slipped toward death.

"I love you...I love you...jesus oh god jesus no...I love you...ah baby...I love you...."

And though I had expected this day, dreaded it, for almost ten years, I was simply unprepared for it. I didn't want him to die; I wanted him with me now, right here, right now.

Forever.

I had considered the option before. In my darkest moments I had wondered if, when the time came, I would be selfish enough to condemn Carl to the same endless highway I had traveled the last thirty-five years. And I had told myself no; his life was sacred to me, and its end would be just that. The end.

Well, that was another fucking lie, wasn't it?

"ANYBODY sittin' here?" the gravelly voice inquired. I looked up from my third Musso and Frank martini and saw Joe standing over me, gesturing at my otherwise empty booth.

"No. I'm all alone, Joe."

Without waiting for an invitation, Joe slid into the seat, his white shirt crisp, his bowtie perfect, his hair as black as shadow. He looked the same on that summer day in 1995 as he had the day Todd Benning ordered my lunch.

"That's the problem with it," he nodded.

I chewed on my olive.

"Problem with what?" I asked him, barely interested in making conversation with anybody anymore.

"Eternity," he shrugged. "So few people really want to spend it with you."

I stopped chewing. Joe leaned back in the booth, his eyes unblinking as he looked at me and for the first time I found myself wondering just how old he really was.

"You sent the invitation?"

He nodded in a matter-of-fact way. I felt anger welling up inside of me and I resisted the temptation to shatter my martini glass and slash his fucking throat with the shards. Instead, I just looked at the tablecloth and lost myself in its pure white linen.

"Why?" I finally asked.

He absently rearranged the salt and pepper shakers on the table, lining them up with the ashtray in some mysterious pattern known only to waiters.

"Figured you needed the help. You looked pretty upset that day. What was it, ten, fifteen years ago?"

I shook my head, smiling wryly.

"Forty, Joe. Forty years."

He let out a soft whistle.

"Whew. Time flies when you're having fun," he smirked, nodding at the empty restaurant, quiet as a tomb. Its heyday had long passed and most of the employees had been let go. But not Joe; Joe, it seemed, would be here forever.

"How long has it been for you?" I asked, finishing the last of my martini.

"Does it matter?" he countered, gesturing to the bartender for another round. "Does it really matter to you?"

I thought about it for a moment. Sudden tears burned my eyes as I pulled Carl's letter from my pocket and slammed it on the table in front of him.

"Yes. Yes it goddamned well does."

As I left the restaurant for the last time, I glanced at the TV over the bar as the bartender flipped the channels. Something must have been wrong with the cable, because he was getting nothing but snow.

THE morning after Carl's first death, I woke up in the living room with a sinus headache. I made my way into the bathroom, found the sun block exactly where I'd left it the day before and slathered it on as I hunted for some Advil, the only thing that seemed to work for me. I'd considered doing a commercial for them but I couldn't imagine they'd be too excited about my testimonial:

Four out of five immortal bloodsucking parasites recommend Advil for your headache pain!

—so I hadn't pursued it too seriously. As I looked into the mirror at the same perfectly chiseled, antiseptic face I'd regarded every day for longer than I cared to recall, I saw that Carl's bed was empty.

It all came back in a flood of memory. His convulsions, his fear, the frightening feeling of life leaving his thin form. And the taste of his blood on my tongue.

He was alive.

"Carl!" I shouted, practically laughing. "Carl?!"

I hurried through the house, expecting to find him in his studio, hard at work on a new painting, the first in what would surely be a long, long series. But the studio was empty, his paintbrushes drying in their jar, and on the easel, pinned to a blank canvas, was a folded note. I took it down and was about to unfold it when I heard Tom barking outside. I moved to the window and looked into the blue light of early dawn.

There, romping naked on the sand with our dog, was my Carl.

I had bled him carefully, taking just enough to let him slip into unconsciousness, before I pushed myself into his thin body. The teeth in my penis were sharp and precise, biting quickly into the raw, emaciated flesh of his rectal cavity, and as I came, shooting the semen which would genetically alter his body, I had cried. For instead of the skeleton I saw beneath me, I had imagined him as he had been.

And as he was now, on the beach below.

Gone were the lesions, the rashes, the bedsores. His body had filled out again, bones hidden away by sinewy muscles, his face lean and strong without even a trace of the stark gauntness the disease had brought to him. His beautiful ass was firm and flexing with his exertions; his plump cock swung between his marbled thighs, nestled in a crop of dark fur. The ocean breeze blew his thick, shining hair around his head like a fiery halo.

He was laughing.

I couldn't speak for a moment, so mesmerized was I by his resurrection. He picked up a stick and threw it into the waves. Tail wagging, barking insanely, Tom dove in after it and Carl turned back toward the house.

When he saw me standing on the studio balcony, he froze for a moment, and it was almost as if he didn't recognize me.

"Good morning!" I called to him, tears pouring down my face. "Good fucking morning!"

He finally smiled. As he raised his hand to wave, the sun appeared on the horizon, burning a golden path across the purple sky

—*the sun block was exactly where I'd left it*—

"Carl!!" I screamed, panic clutching my chest like a vise.

He just kept waving up at me, his smile getting bigger and bigger.

"No, Carl! Come back in here! Do you hear me?! Get back inside!"

The sun rose higher in the distance, red waves riding the tide toward the beach.

"Carl!!!"

The first ray of sunlight hit him on the legs and the muscles in his powerful calves separated from the bone, turning to a wet, stringy mass which simply liquefied under the weight of his body. He dropped to his knees, which also dissolved on contact with the sand, and raised the charred, smoking bones which had been his arms into the air as the sun pulled away from the edge of the world, taking its rightful place in the sky.

He cocked his head and looked at me—

—*what the fuck*—

the moment before the rest of his body exploded in a spray of red.

I dropped to the floor and vomited, tasting my own bile mixed with his blood. Tom galloped out of the ocean, proudly carrying his retrieved stick back to where Carl had stood. He was confused for a moment, unsure where his master had gone, but as he sniffed the wet ground around him his tail dropped between his legs. He buried the stick under what had once been my lover and laid down with a whimper.

Tom didn't move from that spot for three days.

THERE was very little traffic on the drive up to San Luis Obispo, and I found my mind drifting back to Joe, sitting across from me at the restaurant. I wondered what he was doing just then. I wondered whether or not he felt the same loneliness I did. I wondered what madness had driven him to embrace eternity.

And I wondered if he had read Carl's letter.

I had sat numbly in front of the television set, blindly flipping channels for twenty four hours straight, before I could summon the courage to even pick the note up off the studio floor. When I finally did, I held it between my hands like I was praying, trying to feel something he might have left behind, some tangible evidence that I had once loved and been loved. But there was nothing except ink, and the words he had wanted me to read.

I couldn't jump was all it said.

This time, I didn't pack. I closed up the house, dropped Tom off at a neighbor's, and headed north.

Had he always known? Had my lies and deceits been only for my own benefit? Had I awakened before him, told him how to apply the sun block, the contact lenses, how to mix the protein, would he have listened?

I tell myself yes, because it is too difficult for me to contemplate the alternative; that he had come to terms with his own mortality, had faced and welcomed death, and that my own selfishness had dragged him back to this life for a brief, tantalizing moment, only to destroy him again.

And in the darkest place of what remains of my soul, I keep an even more painful thought: he had known about but ignored the protections, the sun block, the food, choosing death over the horrors of eternal life.

I pushed the accelerator as far down as it would go and narrowed the distance to my final destination.

YOU probably know the rest of the story. God knows every paper in the country picked it up and last I heard there were no fewer than eight unauthorized biographies in the stores. But just to set the record straight, let me tell you the truth.

For once.

First of all, the body they pulled from that classic model T-Bird wasn't mine. Turns out the William Morris Agency bought The Center sometime during the high-finance eighties, and they had a vested interest in at least keeping my name alive, for reasons that I'm sure are obvious to you.

It all started when some theater owner in Reseda began playing *Daniel Boone 2000* to packed houses at midnight on Saturdays. "Entertainment Tonight" did a piece on it and suddenly the phenomenon spread across the country. At one point, no less than six hundred screens were showing the damn movie, making it one of *Variety's* Top Ten Grossing Films of the year.

Suddenly, it was hip to be a Paul Douglas fan. *People* called for an interview, *Entertainment Weekly* wanted a cover story and *Rolling Stone* planned an entire Hot Issue around me. They started rerunning "Upstairs with Ed" on MTV and I recently heard that there's going to be an "Off the Top" convention this summer in Chicago.

I'm Flavor of the Month again. Go figure.

So when I showed up at The Center depressed, suicidal, and ready to walk into the next available sunrise, Dr. Carrington was on an emergency conference call to my agents within minutes.

A focus study group showed that my name was worth more dead than alive, so they simply found a guy my size, knocked him unconscious, and riveted his hands to the wheel of my car. By the time he woke up, it was too late; he was already dead, wrapped around a tree ten miles out of Oxnard.

Lucky stiff. We don't have that option up here in Obispo. They need us too badly.

I've had four clients already this week.

During the first few procedures I performed, I tried to warn my kills what was probably going to happen to them; the grief, the pain, the pitfalls of eternal life, that sort of thing. But by the time I'm brought into the operating room, they've already been drugged and anything I say or do will probably be processed as a dream which will haunt them for the rest of their lives. Something from their past, no doubt, possibly with a guest appearance by their first love or their favorite breakfast cereal.

It's not so bad here, really. The rooms are small but comfortable, and although we're not allowed outside—most of us came here wishing to die and the management don't want any suicide attempts in the midday sun—some of my neighbors are very interesting.

Rudolph Valentino lives across the hall, next door to John Belushi. Marilyn Monroe and Jayne Mansfield are roommates and sometimes they fight like cats and dogs. James Dean pretty much keeps to himself; one of the nurses told me he's been rereading the same Kerouac book since he checked in. I'm pretty sure I saw Elvis this morning at breakfast and I heard they've been holding a place for Dick Clark for years.

I often think about Carl. I still miss him very, very much, but I long ago realized that he made the right choice. I know he'd hate it here.

There's a TV in every room.

.

AMSTERDAM

SIMON SHEPPARD

LATE afternoon, when things change.

Tall, maybe six-five. Thin, almost skinny. Not bad looking, but short of handsome. Just his type. The thin man looked at him and stroked his crotch.

At this time of day, the Web wasn't crowded. Maybe two dozen men, most stopping by on their way home from work. For a drink, a quick fuck, shelter from the raw February wind. All sorts: older guys still in good shape; younger guys with hungry eyes; tired men significantly past their prime. A chubby guy with a North English accent joking with the barboy. A Japanese tourist still gripping his indecipherable guidebook.

Everyone in the bar's rear room was staring up at the video monitor, where a blond hunk shoved his latex-gloved hands up the butts of two kneeling men with wide-open assholes. Everyone except the thin man, who was staring not at the monitor, but straight at him. He felt his crotch swelling against his winter camouflage pants. Staring straight back, he grabbed at his thickening dick.

The thin man walked to the stairs and went up toward the darkroom, never looking back.

He gulped down the rest of his Dommelsch and headed for the stairs. Just above his head, the blond hunk was still punch-fucking a stretched-out hole.

Up the stairs, opposite the direction of the "Exit" arrow, white diagonal against black wall. Out one door, then back inside through another. At first the darkroom was impenetrably black, but in seconds his eyes had adjusted. The dim shape of the thin man was leaning against a wall directly in front of him, waiting. For a few long seconds, neither man moved.

The thin man turned, walked down a dark hallway. He followed. At the end of the hallway, a room with a toilet on the left, a still darker room on the right. The thin man leaned against an invisible wall. They were inches apart. They could feel each other's hot breath. The thin man reached down with both hands, grabbed both dicks, squeezed.

He put his hand around the thin man's narrow waist. Slid his hands beneath his shirt. Scabbed-over nipples. Amsterdam, he thought, must be the tit-work capital of the world. The thin man let go of his cock and raised his hands behind his head. He slid his hands to the thin man's belt buckle, started to undo it. The thin man pushed his hips forward and moaned.

Freed of jeans and briefs, the thin man's average-sized, uncut dick stood stiffly out. From somewhere down below, the muffled beat of neo-disco. He grabbed the thin man's cock with his left hand and stroked, sliding foreskin over dickhead. His right hand found the guy's ass and gave it an exploratory slap. The thin man groaned for more. He grabbed the thin man's hips and turned him around so he was facing the wall, hands still behind his head. He slapped the guy around in earnest now, each whack of hand against flesh echoing through the darkroom. The thin guy writhed appreciatively, pushing his butt out for more. When he reached around for the thin man's cock, it was dripping wet.

He shoved the man over to a bench and forced him down onto his knees. Not "forced," really, since the thin man quickly lowered his head to the bench and hungrily shoved his butt in the air. Even in the room's near-darkness, the white flesh of his ass glowed softly. A dark crack down the middle. The rich, slightly revolting smell rose to his nostrils like an aphrodisiac.

The action had gathered a small crowd: a couple of the older guys, the Japanese tourist. He'd built a rhythm, whacking one butt-cheek, then the other, then a slap right down the moist, hot crack. Somebody's hand reached out to the bottom boy's ass. Rude motherfucker. He pushed the hand away, reached between the skinny thighs and grabbed hold of hard dick. WHACK! The thin guy pulled away. He pulled him back by the dick. Slapped him again, hard.

"Pull your pants up and follow me to a *hokje*." He headed down the hall to one of the small, dark cubicles with locking doors. The thin man followed him in. He closed the door and clicked the lock shut.

A few minutes later, the lock clicked open. The thin man walked out alone. The Japanese tourist, still hungry, hesitated for a minute, then walked in. Tripped over something on the floor. Something heavy and soft. Bent down, peered into the darkness. Opened his mouth and screamed.

But by then the thin man was gone, fading into the gray drizzle shrouding the Sint Jacobsstraat.

Late afternoon. I'm walking down the Sint Jacobsstraat, across the Damrak to the Warmoesstraat, past Mister B and the Argos, over to where the tourists feed the pigeons on Dam Square. I stop for a paper cone of frites. I'm not hungry, of course, but the hot fried potatoes with mayonnaise get the taste of blood out of my mouth.

Amsterdam is a brown city. A brown, old city. And I was old when these buildings were new. A tired, cold city. As I am tired and cold.

I've been careless. Leaving that boy in the bar back there. Unforgivably careless. In all my years, my centuries, I've never done such a thing. They're going to get me. Now they're going to get me. And I don't care.

HE walked into the Argos. Past the chains hanging from the ceiling, the satanic animal head hanging by the bar. Just past midnight, not yet crowded. Down the steep, familiar stairs to the darkroom in the basement. Plenty of guys hanging around already. That one, the one illuminated by the light from the stairway, he looked interesting. Faintly familiar. Tall, maybe six-five, and thin, almost skinny. Sharp cheekbones, eyes hidden in shadows; he would do.

He walked over to the thin man, looked up at his face. The thin man's expression gave nothing away. He reached up, stroked the thin man's hair. The thin man put his hands behind his head and leaned back against the wall. As though he was waiting to get blown. Or slapped. He reached down, undid the guy's zipper. Already hard. "Come to a cabin," he said, in English, to be safe. The leaning man didn't move. He repeated it in Dutch, but there still was no response. He slapped the guy's hard dick. The tall, thin man writhed in pleasure, and he did it again, harder. "Yes," the man said. "Ja."

He grabbed the thin man's dick and pulled him into one of the wooden cubicles, locking the door behind them. He unbuckled the man's belt, pulled his jeans down to his knees, then ran his hand up a thin, solid inner thigh till he felt the soft, warm ballsac against his fingers. He flicked a forefinger at the man's balls. The man moaned and shoved his crotch forward. He slapped the man's balls with the palm of his hand. "Good?" he asked. The man nodded. "Poppers?" Another nod. He shoved a small brown bottle under the man's nose, then took a hit himself.

Within seconds, they were tearing at one another, kissing so hard that he could taste blood in his mouth. He unbuttoned his fly, pulled out his dick, grabbed a cock in each hand, and stroked. The thin man grabbed him by the throat, tracing his veins with cold fingertips.

My hands are on his throat. My lips are on his neck. I want to strike, I'm ready to bite down. I can taste him. I can taste him already. And then he moves his hand from my cock to the back of my head, presses my face into the hot hollow of his neck. In a husky voice he whispers, "That's it. That's right, fucking kill me, man," And I'm overcome, not by feelings of lust, but by sudden, irrational tenderness. It's so unexpected. Unasked for. I don't want to leave him there. I don't want to leave him at all. I run my tongue from his neck, along the hard ridge of his jawline, over his stubbly chin, back into the warm, sweet cave of his waiting mouth.

THE thin man, Theo, hurried from the bar. "Hey, wait up." The boy who said he wanted to die. Theo hesitated, then turned around. In the dim light of the cold, windy street, the boy looked thin and fragile. "Where're you off to?" The boy spoke Dutch with a Slavic accent.

"Home."

"Mind if I come along?"

"What's wrong with your home?"

"Okay, okay, sorry." The boy turned to go. The seat of the boy's jeans was thoroughly ripped-up. The flesh of his ass looked tender and pale.

"You really want me to kill you?" Theo's voice was tender, too. Tender and pale.

"I want you to take me home with you."

"My bike's over there."

"Mine, too."

They unchained their bicycles.

"I live over by the Ostkerk." Suddenly, despite his hunger, all Theo wanted to do was sleep, sleep with this boy in his arms.

"Let's go, then."

And they pedaled off into the black, raw, welcoming night.

It's morning now. The boy is curled up, asleep beside me. How did this happen, this compromise, this need? How could I have let him get this far, come into my apartment, into my life?

Christ, I'm starving.

MILOS woke, stretched like a cat, smiled at Theo. "Coffee?"

"None made."

"I'll do it. You just stay there." Milos' skin was translucently pale, revealing blue veins coursing with blood.

Milos climbed out of bed and walked off to the kitchen. Theo couldn't take his eyes off the boy's ass, the way skin and muscles shifted as he moved. The boy was fleshy, not plump exactly, but fleshy, as though he were happy with his body, at home in his body. Milos' dick was still hard as he switched on the coffee maker.

"It'll take a few minutes. Come back to bed." I could do it now, Theo thought. I could do it right now.

Milos bounded back toward the bed, his dick bouncing crazily. He kneeled by the side of the bed, grabbed Theo's wrists and guided the thin man's hands to his throat. Theo's hands slipped around his neck. He bent to kiss Theo's lips. "Squeeze harder," he whispered into Theo's mouth. The grip grew tighter. He wrapped his hands around Theo's hands and pressed them into his flesh. His dick had gotten so hard it almost hurt. His breath was coming in gasps. Blood pounded in his head.

Theo was out of bed now, kneeling on the floor, kneeling between Milos' naked thighs, his knee pressing hard into the Slavic boy's soft balls and hard dick. He pressed Milos' head back till the boy arched his back, groaned, fell backward against the cold floor. Theo threw himself onto Milos' squirming body, dick against dick, hands still around his new lover's throat. He took Milos' lower lip between his teeth, bit down hard, made blood flow. The dark, metallic taste filled their mouths like a sudden shock. They came, both came, brutally, desperately, ecstatically. Theo loosened his grip, stroked Milos' beautiful face, wiped the tears from his eyes.

"I'm hungry," Milos said.

"You're welcome to the kitchen, but I'm afraid you won't find much to eat."

While the naked boy was rummaging around in the hollow cabinets, Theo reached for the remote and switched on the TV. A too-handsome blond man was reading the news. "Police are still searching for the killer of a man who was found murdered in the dark room of a popular gay leather bar this week...."

None of this is simple. I wanted it to be simple, the relationship of predator and prey. Instead, I have this...this boy here, someone to—God, I don't know, look after?—just when I've become so tired, so fucking weary. Just when I've begun to sow the seeds of my own destruction.

Unless, of course, he himself is part of the process.

ON the third morning, they were lying entwined in each other's arms when the doorbell rang. Theo struggled out of bed and pulled on a thick woolen robe.

Pieter was at the door. "Mind if I come in? It's freezing out here."

"It's not a convenient time, Pieter. I'm sorry, but you could have called first."

"Who's this, then?" Pieter's pale blue eyes were staring at Milos, who'd gotten out of bed and was standing a few feet behind Theo, naked, one hand loosely cupped around his dick.

"Pieter, this is Milos." Theo's voice was dead. "Milos, Pieter."

"Is he one of us then? Have you had him yet? No?" Pieter walked over to Milos, reached for the boy's ass, and kissed him on the cheek. "Well, don't worry dear, he will."

Pieter turned on his heel, walked out the door, and was gone.

"What did he mean, 'one of us'?" Milos asked while he was pulling on his pants, preparing to go out in search of breakfast.

"Perhaps I should tell you," Theo said. This has gone on long enough, he thought.

I told him. I told him everything. He didn't say a word. I don't even know him well enough to be able to read his face. So I don't know.

He's out now, gone to get some breakfast for himself. He's lucky that his hunger can be assuaged so easily. Has he gone to the police? No, I doubt it. Will he be back? I have no way of knowing. Do I even want him to come back? Outside the windows, the gulls are swirling above the half-frozen canal. Do I even want him to come back?

IT was already early afternoon when Theo heard the click of the key in the lock. Milos locked the door behind himself and just stood there, the chilly light playing on the angles of his face. For a moment they watched each other in silence. Then Milos knelt at Theo's feet, reached into a little bag he was holding, and pulled out an old-fashioned straight razor. He opened the gleaming blade and held it against the skin of his forearm. Looking deep into Theo's eyes, he drew the razor across his flesh, leaving a gleaming red line in its wake. He offered his wound up to the tall, thin man standing above him. Theo leaned down, put his lips to the blossoming flow, and nursed gently. As he sucked at the upwelling blood, he felt the boy's body shudder, tense, then shudder again. It was not till he drew his lips from the wound that he realized that Milos had used his free hand to unbuckle his jeans and take out his cock. His half-hard dick, shiny with cum, still rested in his fingers.

"Had enough?"

"For now," Theo said. "For now."

Milos pressed his hand against the gash to stanch the flow. "I love you," he said.

Theo stared out the window at the flocks of gulls diving, wheeling, diving again.

Sometimes I think back to the great days of Amsterdam. Down by the Montelbaanstoren, desperate men with nothing to lose boarded ships that would take them to the edge of the world. I would watch them sail off, and wonder how they felt as they looked back at the cozy brown city they might never see again. Maybe the way I do when I look into this Slavic boy's eyes.

ANOTHER day passed. Theo was feeling faint with hunger. He offered Milos some of the hashcake he'd bought at the gay *koffieshop*, waited till the boy was asleep, then slipped out and bicycled to the Web. He found a boy that was to his liking, very young, short and slight, with a nose ring and a dazzling smile. It was easy to get him to go to the darkroom, easy to get him into a cabinet, easy to pull the clothes from his body until the boy stood naked before him, thin almost hairless, with a small, almost delicate hard-on. Delicate, that's what he is, Theo thought as he slipped his hands around the boy's thin neck. He knew that this was stupid, doing this here, so soon after the other one. Even so, he pulled the boy closer, till he could feel the boy's body heat, till the skinny young boy began jamming his hard little dick against his leg.

"Please let me suck you," the boy gasped, reaching for Theo's crotch. The naked boy kneeled. Theo watched as the kid opened his fly, gulped down his cock. A thousand miles away. The skinny boy seemed to be a thousand miles away. A bony white shape in the airless gloom. Skinnier even than he was. But not, despite his voracious cocksucking, anywhere near as hungry.

In a few short moments, Theo's hunger was sated.

Milos' heart. I lie here undreaming, watching him sleep. Deep within him, within his fragile, mortal body, his heart pumps, steadily, erotically, sending life through the network of his veins. His heart, his secret heart.

I want to reach inside him, into his soft ass, slide my hand up into him until I grasp his heart, feel its mindless beating. Hold his life in my hands. Feel the coursing of his lifeblood against my fingertips.

But do I want to love him? Do I want him to love me?

"**THE** police were around to my place, asking questions."

"They haven't been here yet."

"They will be." Pieter was sprawled in Theo's living room, sipping strong black coffee. "You're the one, aren't you, Theo? You're the one who did it. Stupid of you."

Theo stared at the square of moonlight on the floor.

"You've ruined a good thing, brought trouble to the rest of us, too." Pieter's pale blue eyes shone in the semidarkness.

"You're angry, then?"

"Not really angry, Theo. But if trouble comes, I won't be there for you, none of us will. You do understand, don't you?"

"Of course I do."

The front door lock clicked open. Milos walked in, arms loaded with groceries.

"Ah, I see the dream boy is home," Pieter sneered.

"Why do you hate me, Pieter? Is it because you're jealous?"

"How wrong you are, boy. I knew Theo long before you arrived on the scene, and I'll know him long, long after you've gone."

"Why, then?"

"Because Theo is acting like a damn fool, and you're a part of that. You're a threat to him. A threat to us all. You think you understand. Maybe you even think Theo loves you. But you understand nothing, nothing at all. You're just a little fool, a young, young fool."

"I think you've said enough." Theo's voice was flat, expressionless, lacking passion, maybe lacking conviction. "I think you'd better go now."

"Maybe I'd better. But when this all comes crashing down, you'll remember what I've said. Though it will be cold comfort to you then, Theo." Pieter smiled grimly. "You may not believe this, but I wish with all my heart that I turn out to be wrong."

He was at the door, wrapping a long woolen cape around his shoulders. "Take good care of Theo, little boy. He's in trouble. Big trouble." He opened the door. The cold night blew in. And then Pieter was gone.

I haven't been able to sleep. I walked the frozen streets till dawn, till mid-morning. My wanderings have led me here, to the Rijksmuseum. To the long hall that leads to The Night Watch, hordes of tourists squinting at Rembrandts. Over here, to one side, almost ignored, hangs The Jewish Bride. It's an astonishing painting, one of Rembrandt's finest. A light seems to glow from within the couple, he placing his hand upon her breast. Over her heart. Their hands meet in unutterable tenderness. The light remains undimmed, through all the years since it was newly made.

And this tenderness, it makes me want to weep. Only I can't weep. Because I'm closed off, forever cast out from the tenderness of this couple, this simple love. And so I can't weep, because I can't feel. Not like they feel. And so whatever else I'm trying to feel is turning to bitterness, to anger. I can see why that man took out a knife and slashed The Night Watch. If I had a knife...

If I had a knife...

"WHERE have you been?" Milos asked. "The police were here looking for you. They said they'd be back later."

Nothing can kill me, because I'm not alive. Not in the way other people are. Not in the way Milos is, warm, feeling, hot blood coursing through his veins, blood that he kneels to offer me. His heart is a work of art, a work of art of unutterable tenderness.

When I told him I had to go, he said he wanted to come with me. To escape. There's no place to escape, I said.

He stripped himself naked for me. His dick was already hard. He begged me to put my hands around his neck. To squeeze hard.

His heart is a fucking work of art.

WHEN the police arrived at the apartment by the Ostkerk, they found the door ajar. They called out; no one was home. They pushed the door open. In the middle of the living room floor was a pool of blood, three, maybe four feet across. It had been shaped into the form of a heart, a wet valentine. The outer edges of the heart were drying to a duller brown, but the center of the heart was still shiny, wet, red.

On the wall above the heart, someone had thumbtacked a postcard to the wall. A reproduction of a painting. A Rembrandt: *The Jewish Bride*.

So fucking tired. So fucking weary. So very, very old.

THE NIGHTWATCH
IS A LONELY VIGIL

KEVIN ANDREW MURPHY

"**SHEAR** it off. All of it." Andrew looked to the monk, whose name he didn't know. The short, fat one with the scissors. They all looked the same anyway. "God must know my grief."

The fat monk smiled and snicked his shears, long as daggers, sharp as teeth, gleaming in the torch light of the underground vault. He stepped forward, eyes glimmering with anticipation. Then he paused, as if uncertain for a moment, and looked to Brother Martin, Andrew's new sponsor and the only monk he recognized.

The old monk only bowed his head and sighed, fingers steepled in an attitude of prayer. Then he looked up and raised one hand, gently waving in disagreement. "Tut-tut, my good youth. The Lord already knows your grief. Your hair must be shorn to show your submission to the will of God. To give it another meaning would be to show disrespect." He put his hands on the fat monk's shoulders and moved him aside with an indulgent smile, causing him to close the shears with a sharp snick! "Brother Leonard gets ahead of himself anyway. We cannot shear your hair until *after* the sins of your former life are washed away. Are you prepared for that, Squire Andrew?"

Andrew nodded, head bowed.

"Strip him," Brother Martin ordered then, gesturing abruptly. At once, a dozen hands came forth from the darkness, sleeved and cassocked, fat and thin, fumbling at his belt, grabbing his tunic and pulling it over his head, cutting the cord which held up his hose and pulling the leggings down. The cold of the vault bit at his skin, his manhood drawing up at the touch, and after a flurry of dark cloth, the monks stepped back, leaving him naked in the middle of the underground baths.

Water dripped and echoed in the shadows, the cowled monks standing around him like a murder of crows, eyes glittering. Wordless, Brother Martin pointed to a wooden tub, and Andrew went and stepped into the middle. A tall monk, gaunt as Death, busied himself with a kettle, removing it from the fire and adding its contents to a cauldron with a hiss and the stench of sulfur, while the other shadowed figures readied pitchers and ewers, silent as the gargoyles which leered from the cornices of the pillars overhead.

"Squire Andrew," Brother Martin intoned, voice echoing through the vault, "are you now ready for the water to wash away your former life, as God sent the deluge to wash away the sins of the world?"

Andrew nodded, feeling a tear slide down his cheek. Sir Geoffrey. He had always said he would be here....

It was better to forget anyway, or at least less painful. He bit his lip, not wanting the tears to start again, or the monks to see him so unmanned. "I am ready."

Andrew didn't see the old monk signal; his first notice was when the water struck him, cold as ice, drenching him, and he opened his eyes, sputtering, to see a shadowed figure with a wooden pail. A second stepped forward then with another bucket, dousing him with the icy chill, wetting down his hair and beard till they ran with streams of water.

Then the tall monk came forward with a fat-bellied copper ewer and poured warm, steaming water over him, the hot stream making his hair and beard stink with old grease and tears and the hellish scent of brimstone. "Scrub him," commanded Brother Martin. "Wash away his sins. We're not baptizing an infant, you know, and a young man has had occasion to gather sins aplenty."

The hands surrounded him, with brushes and rags, scrubbing and scouring him till his skin nearly bled, grabbing and ducking him in pools of hot and cold, sulfurous and fresh, till he thought he had died and gone to Hell and the fiends had taken hold of him.

The next thing he knew, he was back in a chair. The fat monk stood over him, quietly snicking his shears, Brother Martin on the other side. "Are you ready to show your obedience to God?" the old monk intoned, torch fire in his eyes, his voice conjuring forth all the fury of Heaven and Hell.

Andrew closed his eyes and bit his lip, remembering Sir Geoffrey and how he had said this moment would be. "I am."

"Then it is done," pronounced Brother Martin. "Shear away his beard and wash and oil him, so he may go before God with the clean and handsome face of a newborn. But of his hair take but one lock to show his obedience."

The fat monk set to work with the scissors, and Brother Martin glanced over his shoulder, stern but kind. "My sympathies to you, my son, but if you wish to shear your hair for grief, you will do it after you've accepted your oath, not before. I will have no confusion while you are in my keeping."

"Yes Father," Andrew said.

The fat monk giggled. "Careful. You don't want me nicking you."

Andrew closed his eyes, unmoving, feeling the steel of the razor scrape against his throat and thinking of the blood, the bright red blood, and the fall. And the cold silence and darkness.

It had all happened so quickly. One moment his liege, Sir Geoffrey, riding proud for all to see, torches flickering and pennants fluttering across the parade grounds. Sir Geoffrey, the Dark Knight, named not for a blank shield, as with the other knights of that name, but for his custom of receiving challenges solely between the hours of dusk and dawn, and never stepping abroad during daylight, strange as that might be. Sir Geoffrey, the brave and handsome, the hero of the Crusade, only man of his company to return.

Then the next moment, a crack and a snap. A shield buckle giving way, a lance tip splintering askew, a blossom of bright red blood on a white tabard. And then Sir Geoffrey, falling to the dirt of the tilt yard, a wooden shaft driven through his chest. A length of rotten wood and a bit of frayed leather doing the deed that neither Saracen steel nor Moorish sorcery had been able to accomplish.

They had laid him out in his pavilion, and later, the chapel, Sir Geoffrey, the Tortured, who had gone to church each night without fail, yet ever since his return from the Holy Land had denied himself the blessing of Communion, refusing even to dip his fingers in the font when he paused to cross himself, as if afraid his very touch might in some way contaminate the blessed water. A strange habit which caused folk to whisper, though in all other ways he had been the most perfect of knights and the most righteous of men.

Andrew had wept while the priests argued as to the disposition of his liege's body, and, it was to be inferred, his soul. It was true that he'd been a Crusader, and as such, the Pope had assured that all his past sins were forgiven and washed clean in the sight of God. But of his deeds since his return, and the sins which no doubt weighed his heart and conscience—for why else would a sane man refuse Holy Communion, or even to touch the water of the font?—what of those? How could they be absolved if he had not made confession or received Last Rites?

In the end, Sir Lionel, whose rotten lance had slain him, had sworn at the priests and bought a sheaf of Indulgences, sufficient to grease the bars of Heaven for all but the blackest of souls—and such could never be said of Sir Geoffrey, even though he always dined alone in his chambers and never broke bread with other men. For all that, Sir Geoffrey had been the kindest of men and the most generous of hosts, and as Sir Lionel had said, impious but honest, if God held to any higher standards, then Heaven was deserted but for the saints, and a number of them should think seriously about packing their bags.

And through it all, Sir Geoffrey had lain there, beautiful and incorruptible, looking as if he were nothing more than asleep, the flies refusing to touch him. The priests had said that this was a sign of God's favor and his honor, Sir Lionel's chirurgeon only that it was most odd, but whatever the cause, they were still in agreement on the fact that Sir Geoffrey was dead, and would ride no more.

Black was the color of death and mourning, and though the clothes were new, the shade was all too familiar. The monks dressed Andrew in black hose and slippers and a clinging shirt of finest lawn, Brother Martin droning on about it being a symbol of his death to the world, and Andrew nodded in agreement, but refused to let the tears show. Sir Geoffrey, always so brave, would be ashamed if he were here now and saw his squire cry like some woman, even for the death of his own lord.

A white shift was next, white for purity and innocence. Even if that innocence be lost. Then a red cloak, red for nobility, and for blood. Blood shed willingly for God and Church.

He had tried to staunch the flow. He had run forward, falling to his knees, still bruised, and he'd held his hands around the shaft, trying to stem the crimson geyser. But it would have been simpler to hold back the tide. Simpler and far less futile. Andrew could still feel the blood on his hands, dark and wet and cold as seawater, as if his beloved lord had been dead long before the lance tip had even touched him, though the chirurgeon had said such odd perceptions were common in cases of shock and nothing he should trouble himself over.

The white belt of chastity was last. Brother Martin droned on about its symbolism and his responsibilities, but Andrew bit his lip and knew its truth. He would never touch another. Not so long as he lived.

"Are you ready to begin your vigil?" the old monk asked, the question startling him into awareness of where he was.

"Of course." Andrew shook his head. "Please, lead on."

Brother Martin nodded. "Certainly, my child. I know this must be hard for you. Coming back to the Church again, and under such different circumstances. But it was your liege's wish that you be knighted on this day, and though he cannot stand as your sponsor, he is here. They placed his slab but this afternoon."

"He is here?"

Brother Martin nodded again, ushering him into the chapel. "He is. You are to speak to no one and contemplate only your duties to God on this night, but I don't believe Our Lord will mind you taking a moment to pay your respects. Sir Geoffrey swore he would be here, and a true knight is good to his word, no matter what the obstacle."

He attempted to guide Andrew down the aisle, but Andrew could see the sarcophagus at once and he quickly outstepped the older man. Atop the slab lay a marble effigy: his liege, Sir Geoffrey, reclining as befit a crusader, sword at the ready, poised to rise again.

Andrew looked down. "I am sorry, my Lord. The buckle—" The words caught in his throat, and the hot tears broke free, beginning to wash down his cheeks. He turned away lest the old priest see him.

Brother Martin, at his side again, put a hand on his shoulder. "Hush, my child, and do not shy away from death. There is no dishonor or unmanliness in weeping at a graveside, especially of one so beloved as your liege. Make your peace, then come to the altar and you may begin your vigil."

Andrew nodded thanks, and the old priest moved away. He turned back to the effigy upon the slab, marveling at how truthfully the sculptor had captured his liege's likeness. Here the fine brow, there the high arch of his cheeks, and around his eyes the fine lines that gathered together when he laughed. All transfigured into snowy marble, as lily fair as Sir Geoffrey's true skin, though the lips were white as well, pale and bloodless, though otherwise like as like.

"Oh, my liege..." Andrew leaned down and kissed the stone of the effigy, though the lips were hard, cold and unresponsive.

After a long moment and a final sob, Andrew stood up, wiping his tears away on the sleeve of the white tabard. "I know you are watching me, Sir Geoffrey. I just wish.... Well, you know what I wish. Sleep well."

He leaned down and gave the effigy a second kiss, chaste and delicate, then turned and walked up the nave of the church, brushing at the wetness on his cheeks.

Brother Martin had arranged his things upon the steps of the altar, his gear and the responsibilities of knighthood. The armor and sword, a legacy from his father. The tabard and banner, lovingly picked out in red and gold, the handiwork of his mother and sisters. And the shield, painted with his crest, the gift he knew he was to have received from Sir Geoffrey.

At the sight of it, the tears came again, hot and womanish, but the old priest said nothing, only allowed him to weep, then wipe his cheeks and take up his sword.

"You must either stand or kneel for your vigil, Squire Andrew, though I will admit, I am too old and infirm to do the same. If you will allow it, I will simply sit and watch from the foremost pew while you make your peace with God and reflect upon your responsibilities." He paused. "I have attended you since Communion this morning. You have not broken fast or otherwise impinged upon your vows?"

"I have not. Except..." He glanced to the shield, then back to Sir Geoffrey's crypt, then turned back to the priest, feeling the hot tears running down his face.

"Except you have had your thoughts of duty disturbed by grief." Andrew nodded and the old priest waved in benediction. "It is forgiven, my son. On this night, you must reflect upon all that it is to be a knight. To reflect on death is but part of that, and grief gives us an understanding. In this, you will be far more prepared than most young men." He paused. "Now say your prayers, and I will sit and watch so that you do not falter in your responsibilities, or be tempted by sleep."

Brother Martin touched his fingers to Andrew's brow. "Bless you, my child, and may the Lord give you strength."

"Thank you, Father."

Still weeping, Andrew took up his sword and held it before him in the manner of a cross, tip down, then genuflected to the altar. "Hearken we beseech Thee, O Lord, to our prayers, and deign to bless with the right hand of Thy Majesty this sword with which Thy servant desires to be girded, that it may be a defense of churches, widows, orphans, and all Thy servants against the scourge of pagans, that it may be the terror and dread of all evildoers, and that it may be just in both attack and defense."

The words echoed through the vault of the church, the high candles about the altar flickering, and Andrew looked upon the Crucifixion and the Passion of Christ, seeing the red blood flow down, almost black in the dim light.

Such a senseless death. Sir Geoffrey had survived far worse, had told tales of Moorish sorcerers and desert witches, dark magicians whose hell-spawned arts had killed all the other men of his company. Of how he had hidden in crypts, watching as ghouls and nightgaunts and the cold dead had fed upon his fallen comrades, and how he had slain the accursed sorcerers who had wrought the deed through the power of their unholy alliance.

And he'd said that he'd be there, to stand vigil beside Andrew, to give him strength to take the vows of a knight. Sir Geoffrey, the brave and handsome, with his pale skin and blood-red lips.

Sir Geoffrey had come home an invalid, dressed in rags, tatters of his former glory, hidden inside a black coach like a corpse inside the contagion wagon, frightened by the light and refusing even to look upon the sun's glory, his fear and pain the legacy of the sorcerers' foul arts and the crypts where he'd hidden. The children had sung songs about him, mocking his state and dreading it all the same, until shushed by their mothers, and, Andrew remembered, with shame, he had been one of those children, not understanding the honor and goodness of the man who shut himself away in his castle, or the horrors he had suffered in defense of the Church, the dreadful things which he'd spoken of only in passing, and even then seldom.

But after a long while sequestered in his family home, Sir Geoffrey had come forth, as beautiful and handsome a knight as he had been when he had left for the Holy Land, and, the women whispered, seemingly untouched by his trials and the passage of years. And he had called for a new squire, a replacement for Douglas, who had fallen in the Crusade.

Andrew didn't know why Sir Geoffrey had chosen him. There were lads who were stronger, or of better family, or who had more natural talent when it came to the sword. But it hadn't mattered. Of all the boys presented, Sir Geoffrey had chosen him and had taught him all of the arts of war and the code of chivalry that a true knight should know.

And Andrew had failed him. A snapped buckle....

The stone of the church floor was hard beneath his bended knee. Andrew looked down, seeing the cross shape of his sword hilt, and chastised himself. He was to think upon the glory of God, and what it was to be a knight, not himself. And yet the prayers...

Kindness to widows and orphans. Andrew's own father had perished in the Crusade, when Andrew was but a baby, and he had known no father until Sir Geoffrey had taken him in and shown him what it was to be a man. He, Andrew, a poor younger son, with little to call his own save his father's second-best arms and armor. His mother naught but a poor widow, kept on but at the whim of her eldest son.

That was what it meant to be a knight. To show that kindness. Not to seek glory or title, but to tend to the meek and wretched, and, if possible, give them heart and teach them how to be brave.

Glong! The church bells began ringing, their tones dark and dolorous in the heights of the church. *Glong! Glong! Glong!*

They had wrung the church bells for Sir Geoffrey's death, and again at his funeral. Rung them for death and the breaking of hearts.

Andrew wept, and remembered what Sir Geoffrey had said. To be a knight meant to weep for lost comrades and to keep their memory alive, so God would know that they had not died in vain.

Glong! Glong! Glong! Glong! Glong! Glong! Glong! Glong!

Midnight. The darkest part of the vigil was upon him, and in the darkness behind him, Andrew heard a whisper and a sigh.

He glanced back, but only saw old Brother Martin, propped against the corner of the pew, eyes closed, snoring gently.

Andrew smiled. Sir Geoffrey had told him the same tale of his own vigil, of how the priest had fallen asleep as well. And he'd promised that he would not, for though Andrew might be tempted to sleep, Sir Geoffrey would not let him, would not let him shame himself in that manner.

Andrew closed his eyes, leaning upon the cross of his sword. The defense of churches...

"Open your eyes, Squire. You must be vigilant."

Andrew looked up, startled, then glanced back to Brother Martin. But the old priest's lids were yet shut.

The whisper came again: "Keep your eyes fixed forward, upon your goal. You are here on this night to fix your eyes upon the Lord, and your duties as a knight."

Andrew looked the other way, and there, in the shadows of the nave, he saw Sir Geoffrey, pale and wan, dressed in his arms and armor as befit a knight, as they had buried him.

"Keep your eyes forward, Squire."

Andrew tore his eyes away, looking upon the altar, and the candles, and the Crucifixion. "Are you..."

"Hush boy." The voice was Sir Geoffrey's, stern but loving. "A knight always keeps his word, and you are under a vow to keep your eyes and your thoughts upon God. Unless your lips open to utter a prayer, let them remain silent."

There was a long moment where no words were spoken, and the only sound was the echo of the vault, and the light tink! of Andrew's sword point grinding against the granite of the church floor. Then Sir Geoffrey's voice came again. "Yes, Andrew. I am dead. But a true knight always keeps his vows, and in truth, I am no different than how you knew me. The Moorish sorcerers and their witches stole my death, denying me the peace of the grave. But my vows were stronger than their sorceries, and though they barred me from the peace of God's Kingdom, they could not stop me from serving it."

Andrew's lips quavered, and his voice faltered, letting forth only a weak croaking sound.

"Hush boy. Only prayers, and that didn't sound like one. And yes, I am a nightgaunt, one of the cold dead, like the ones I fought, but not like them, for my heart is my own, and I know the power of Right and the True Church." There was a long pause. "I have thought long about why this happened to me, why I have been denied the peace of the grave, even when I lay in it, time and again, but I believe I understand why. God has a plan for all things—never forget that—and while I lay amidst the dead and dying, hiding from the sorcerers and nightgaunts, I prayed to God. Not for him to spare me or to save me, for that is not a knight's prayer, but just that if he let me survive, I would slay the pagan sorcerers and their fiends, and I would bear witness to the bravery and valor of my comrades, to assure that they had not died in vain."

There was a long silence. "God heard my prayer, and I survived. Not alive, but existing. And I've done my best to fulfill my vow. All know of my company's valor, and the fate of our enemies." Another pause. "The only vow left which gives any meaning to my existence is my vow to you, to stand beside you on this night, and to see you knighted. That, and my first vows, to be a knight of the Church, honest and true to my word."

The candles flickered, ghostly and blue, and Andrew heard a sigh behind him, a sound which made his heart turn to water in his breast. "They know me as dead now, Andrew. As I truly am. I cannot remain here and honor my comrades, or my vow to God. I must go forth as a wandering knight, with only a cross and a blank shield, and there is one thing I must ask you, though I have no right. Will you join me on my lonely road?"

Andrew glanced aside, seeing the ghastly form of Sir Geoffrey standing there, having come up beside him, looking no different than the day he died, or the marble figure on the slab.

"Wha—"

"Do not speak, Andrew, save to answer yea, or nea. Will you join me on my lonely road, to be my fellow and my other? To walk the night with me, and to do what deeds of chivalry and honor that can be done in the realms outside the sight of God? For the night is long and dark, and the road is hard, and I do not know if I can bear this task by myself. The night-watch is a lonely vigil, and there are terrors reserved for those who cannot die." There was a tear on the dead man's cheek, pale as a drop of moonlight. "Forgive me for asking this of you, but I did not think we would be separated so soon, or that I would so soon be forced to go. But I must know: Will you join me, Andrew? Will you become my brother in arms, to fight by my side, and to share my cold bed? Will you give up life for me, as I would for you, if I still had it to give? Will you join me? Yea, or nea?"

Andrew's lip quivered, looking up at the apparition, the ghastly thing, but a ghost with the face that he loved and the only one to ever bring any peace or meaning to his life. "Oh yea," Andrew whispered. "Yea. If you would have me, I would follow you to the ends of the earth and Kingdom Come."

"That is where we will travel." With a ghostly flash and ring of steel, Sir Geoffrey unsheathed his sword. "Bow thy head, Squire Andrew, so I might confer upon you your honors." Andrew did, and the ghost whispered, "With this, my sword, I dub thee Sir Andrew, and charge thee to be ever vigilant, to uphold the Church, and all that is good and righteous, to be the protector of travelers, and the meek and wretched, and any who are in need of thy aid and strength. Be thou a knight!"

The blow came swift and sharp, no mere tap such as Andrew had seen before, but a hard slash to his neck. Andrew felt the warmth of the blood more than the pain, and the next moment Sir Geoffrey was down on his knees beside him. "Forgive me, Andrew." Then he drew him close, and

Andrew saw the sharp teeth of the ghoul, the lamprey's maw of the night-gaunt which his master had become, and, in truth, had always been, for as long as Andrew had known him.

Then the horrid sight was past his vision, and Andrew felt Sir Geoffrey place his lips to the wound on his neck. The nightgaunt's tongue licked the deep gash with a gentleness which would have shocked him had it been anyone else, and as the dead man fed, Andrew knew him to be nothing other than the man he loved.

His instincts shouted for him to flee, to tear away, to escape from the dead thing that held him, or just to cry out and wake the sleeping priest, whose blessed touch would banish the dark abomination his lord had become. But the passion and the tenderness was such that Andrew knew he could not, he could not twice betray and fail the man to whom he owed his life and all that he was. Even if it meant his salvation and soul.

"Oh, Geoffrey," he whispered, tears running down his cheeks, "I forgive you. I forgive you all of it, and if there is any mercy left in Heaven, God will forgive you as well."

Andrew felt the life ebbing out of him, along with his strength, but also a fierce joy and passion as Sir Geoffrey's teeth kissed and tore at his neck. The light faded, the candle flames of the altar diffusing into nothingness, and even the silence faded but for the ring of delirium's sweet song.

And then he lay upon the church floor, feeling cold as the granite, but somehow still conscious, though his heart lay cold within his breast and he could no longer feel even the tingle of blood within his veins.

"Sleep, Sir Andrew," Geoffrey's voice whispered, the sound the only thing in the darkness. "Sleep but three days, as did Our Lord, then rise up. They will lay you out, then bury you, but you will not rest. Three days hence we shall ride forth from this place, to share the road, and whatever pleasure and honor may be left us. Sleep well, my brother, and remember: You shall rise again."

Andrew felt Sir Geoffrey close his sightless eyes, then gently kiss him once upon each lid. Then he was gone.

And Andrew lay upon the floor of the church, cold and still, and reflected upon what it meant to be a knight.

FOREVER OCTOBER

DAVID QUINN

1. MORGAN'S KISS

Even boys have so much fucking hair. That's the first thing that hit me when Morgan's mouth first came down on mine, nearly twenty years ago. His hair was everywhere. We were seventeen and sweating, rebelliously alive. We kissed then the way we wrestled in the subterranean warmth of the hot, body-smelling, padded gym—clutching, pulling, locked, hard, hot.

Two decades later, we were alone again. Not in the gym, but rolling in the dirt off the path up the hill toward the old cemetery where we used to make our rest stop during training. Half the woods we used to run through are littered with boxy little condos now. The boneyard's still virgin.

Morgan held my head in his hands, his grip strong. I wanted to taste his mouth, to wrestle him to the damp ground and get my teeth into him like I did that night, the one night we were together. The one night in my life I did what I felt like, without holding back. Maybe I was still holding onto the past, but more than anything I wanted to be alive with him again. I wanted this.

But as Morgan opened his mouth, something curdled in me, making all the strength drain out of my arms. His gums had receded drastically. He smiled, the flesh dark against the stark whiteness of his teeth, teeth that now seemed one long nerve, one sensory organ in itself.

He laughed at me, not scornfully, but making me feel I should have known better. Within his laugh, there was the sound of a pounding life, like the noise that used to erupt from our guts when we'd break the top of Three Mile Hill. Morgan's laugh hadn't changed since the fall of our last year of high school.

I wanted him inside me again, to bite into him while he fucked me. I wanted to feel his fucking burn me—

But I was startled by his smooth face; no abrasive nub, as I remembered....And he was cold, almost colder than the earth beneath us.

Then he had me in a half nelson, pushing just hard enough to hurt, saying, "It's good that you're resisting; it heats the blood. But you must understand I'm doing this for you, James. You inspired my journey, and now you're coming with me."

Forever running through October was my idea, you see. Morgan was the jock. I was the one who talked him into taking our nightly runs through the cemetery. I was the one with the hard-on for vampires.

That's what the bright bone shape in the dark of Morgan's mouth was. He had gotten his fangs.

2. THE FETISH

Souvenirs don't do it for me. People who file away the flotsam of their lives always seem so sad, like they're reducing their lives to empty clutter. I sound like a judgmental asshole for saying this, don't I? Maybe I am. Or maybe if I had made the kind of life I could have, a life worth hoarding, I'd have troves of cherished junk, too. From high school, I possessed a few choice volumes—I Am Legend, Interview with a Vampire, The Riverside Shakespeare—my wrestling headgear (the dark, coppery bloodstain from the state finals...), and one photograph.

Yes, it was a picture of Morgan and I. If the lore of the children of the night turns out to be true, no one'll ever catch us on film again. I'll describe it for you.

The camera was on the ground. We looked up at two old, faded gravestones from the last century. You can't read the writing, but I believe that the markers signified the resting places of a married couple returned to dust. On top of the stones, two boys frozen in the moment, the night we did it.

We were a pair, fresh, shirtless, in supple, faded jeans, running shoes stained beyond recognition, no socks. We weren't trying to be anything tomorrow, or the next day, we were just there . The graveyard, as I said, was my idea, but Morgan's anarchic touch asserted itself anyway. We crouched, rigid, muscular, hard, perched atop the gravestones like junior gargoyles till the timer ran down and the flash lit up the night. But at the last second, Morgan decided to improve on our design. He pulled on my arm!

There's that grin breaking on his face as he tried to pull me off my perch. I was laughing, too. The muscles across our chests pulled tight, our arms entwined. The camera flash highlighted muscle tone you never find on a man, even an athlete, over the age of twenty. Something turns in me, even now, wanting to touch that flesh again, taste the burning texture of that night, the leaves and grass we dropped our shoes and pants into, everything sharpened by the crisp air. The next morning, or the morning after that, a first frost might snap the graveyard into flat, gray winter, but, that night warm skin collided with a *crack!*

What started out as wrestling became sucking and biting and fucking and pounding....

No one ever found the photograph, not even the first time I was—

No one ever found the photograph. It's inside the heaviest book I own—halfway through the first part of *Henry IV*. I remembered the words from the play, "for when they seldom come, they wished for come," as I shoved the book under my bed. This photograph is the only ephemera I can't abandon because I want to completely obliterate my life.

3. A NEW SKIN

Like hair treatments and suicide, men my age consider the possibility of attending their twentieth high school reunion. I found a clean shirt and my best sweater and went to mine. Under a paper banner that read "Forward '77," some well-meaning volunteers had glitzed-up the room just enough so no one could forget we were in a gym. Catching my reflection in the glass door, I smiled. Morgan and I used to pound through these doors for practice; tonight, I ambled in like the part-time wrestling coach or a terminal grad student shy just one dissertation of a Ph.D.

Did you ever wish you could grow a whole new you? Steal a reptile's gift and stretch new skin over your old bones? Walk away a new man who no one knows, no one judges, for whom no one holds expectations? That's what I was dreaming when I suddenly found myself nursing a warm beer and looking at Jenny White. Where did she get that southern accent? God, she looked like her mother, the poor thing. But I couldn't think about that. She had the face of someone expecting an answer, and I hadn't even listened to the question.

"Customized training and, uh, development," I mustered, hoping the way I sloshed my beer was the right sort of "man with a plan" gesture. She must have asked what I did; what else do people jabber on about at these things?

Jenny, a big, bland overcooked piece of sausage, thought that one over, then her great breasts shook as she spurted and cackled, "Oh, James, you haven't lost your sense of humor, now have you?—You always were pretty strange!"

She started to bray that she was single, too. Something in her eyes glazed over in a way that was altogether wrong. God, she'd gotten just huge. I felt trapped and we weren't even touching.

No, I don't reckon "consulting" was the right answer to, "So, James, you still haven't found yourself a nice little wife," or whatever she had asked. I ripped my gaze away from Jenny's seismic cleavage and turned to go. I saw other men gaping at her like fresh meat, anyway. She'd forget me.

4. UNDERTOW

At some parking party, early into high school, I had pawed Jenny's big ass, and yes, those tits that all the boys I knew made legend. She was a girl in heat. The wrestling room buzzed as bodies hit the mat and crude jokes stunk up the room. If that had been true, why hadn't she settled down to breed entire wrestling teams by now? Perhaps she married early and divorced. Everything falls apart.

Her pussy made my fingers wet. It felt like blood, but it wasn't. Amazed that she could breed, that life would come screaming through that small dark tunnel, I was obsessed with her holes. She told me she would-n't fuck, but she could come if I sucked her nipples, and then she'd jerk me off. Her breasts were full, even then, earning her the name Boom-Boom around the wrestling room.

Oh, she was famous. Wrestlers dedicated push-up drills to her, and when we did push-ups, we didn't just touch our chest to the floor, but we would snake our entire body, inch by inch, along the mat. We got a better work-out. And we got to shout out the name of the Girl of the Week as our groins rubbed the floor, grunting as we pushed off to wind up another. Even Morgan did. I watched him hump the mat. When the room groaned "Boom-Boom!" I heard "Morgan!" like a harsh current in the liquid of my inner ear.

I remember sucking Jenny's nipples, her urging me on, heaving and making little squeaks. She didn't even need to jerk me off, I was getting there from the sucking. Then I lost it. She was whining at me to move back to her tits, but I was sucking her throat, nipping, nibbling, biting. In my head, I saw Morgan's hips pumping the floor, sweating out the push-ups.

"The children of the night," I panted, "breed by the gift of blood."

When her screaming started to hurt my ears, I stopped biting. Her throat was not the bloodiest I'd ever see, but it was pretty bad. Everyone acted like it didn't happen. Except Morgan. That was when Morgan knew it wasn't a joke and asked me to teach him what I knew.

5. I WANNA BE ANARCHY

Now I know whoever began to blare the Fleetwood Mac album over the gym's PA system meant well, but all it did for me was shake me out of my memories with revulsion. I staggered for the exit, dropping my beer like it had suddenly turned to shit in my hand. I didn't want to hurt anybody, you see, to do that here would serve no purpose. But I felt everything closing in, and needed that new skin.

A weaving cluster of dancers were singing "Taken by, taken by the skyyyy," or whatever that Munchkin-voiced woman was wailing. All I had to do is wade through them and I'd be free. At the door, I almost plowed into a young man in the dark. A kid. Instantly, I thought, "I could take him, but not here."

Then he took me.

"I'm not surprised you're blowing outta here, Jim. We always did prefer the Sex Pistols. You up for a night run?"

Fucking Morgan.

He'd hardly changed. While I'd sunk into twenty years of diminished expectations, fucking Morgan seemed primed, a strutting seventeen-year-old! How the hell did his clock stop ticking the summer after high school?

Oh, I was throbbing for that run. I'd been floating around in my head for twenty years and had crashed into a place where I just might touch the ground.

6. NIGHT RUN

"We'll take my truck," I said once we were out of Fleetwood Mac range. But Morgan kept striding in his old way, moving over the grass between the parking lot and the street.

"Let's race from here!" He called without looking back. "Don't tell me the teenage vampire has grown up to be afraid of the dark."

"You know I love it," I called after him, taking a few scuffling jogging steps. I can still run, but Morgan looked like he could fly. Morgan hadn't changed since we hugged at a graduation party—self-consciously, guardedly, an all-too-public goodnight which turned out to be goodbye. Morgan disappeared after high school.

"Come on, old man!"

"I'm doing all right," I lied.

" 'Customized training?' Come on, you can bullshit the bleachers, but not your old wrestling partner...Fuck," Morgan whirled, hopping in a backward-run down the grassy hill, "You were the one who used to talk about 'living by night' and 'seeing forever.' It hurts to see you like this, man." Morgan cast off his shirt and surged to full five-mile pace.

I had always been a fast runner. I broke the finish line every week that last October in high school when we entered all the cross-country races, with Morgan right behind me. But now I was looking at his back, ditching my sweater, then my shirt, heart pounding to burst.

7. FLYING

Till we learn to fly, nothing comes closer to soaring than running naked at night. I don't know where we left our clothes; flight ripped them off us. Every breath scraped my dry throat, and the ground rushed up to collide with my feet, igniting electric needles inside me. But all that pain was good, transporting me through a dark tunnel of brush and trees.

Suddenly, bare branches laced the edges of a huge sky. White markers reflected the moon. I knew where he had led me—our cemetery, refuge of fall nights. Where we first smoked a joint, off-season, where laughter could be as loud as we wanted, where we made offerings of blood and semen to dead witnesses, where we had each other. I still felt it!

Here's how it happened, twenty years ago: I wrestled him down, locking his arms, inhaling his breath while he was under me. I had never felt my cock so full with blood. It made me dizzy. I had been so awkward with soft Jenny, but everything fell into place with hard Morgan. My chest smacked against his and he wrapped around me. All the leg wrestling we had done, thigh muscles throwing each other, had prepared us to throw ourselves into the heat of each other that night. The first burning was our mouths. Like hot smoke had once passed between us from the joint, I was sucking Morgan's blunt beautiful cock, kissing and biting, hungry for him to pour fluid fire for me.

He tasted like blood, and he didn't laugh when I risked telling him I was becoming a vampire. I felt reborn that night, as if I got my new reptile skin, but I had forgotten all about it, walking around dead for years, till now.

8. IN THE BLOOD

It hurt to breathe, but I didn't stop till he did. My bare feet cut the grass, watching him stretch it out, his limbs a blur. Then Morgan stood between gravestones, twelve paces away. His chest was pulsing and his breath was audible, but at least he could speak.

"You know, if you hadn't wasted so much time trying to find a replacement for me, James, you might still be able to kick my ass. We barely ran a mile and you're caving!"

"What do you mean, 'replacement'?" I managed to answer.

"You know what I mean."

"Why didn't you come back?"

"You weren't ready, Jim. You introduced me to the pleasures of the blood, but you didn't dare push far enough. You quit on me. You wimped out."

"What?"

"I was always inspired by you. We only fucked once, but you mentored me, fathered me. Now if you're up to it, I'm ready to return the favor. Come here."

I had tried to replace him so many times. I don't know how he knew it, but he did. No one ever tasted as good as Morgan, though, and I had to let them go cold. Once, I even had to go away for doing it. But that didn't make me stop. That just made me more careful on my night runs. But I don't want to dwell on my failures...

Could I ever feel it with another man? I don't know. I tell people I'm straight, though in these paranoid days, I'm more like some kind of sorry modern temple eunuch. Morgan could change that. What we had together was the best sex-fuck, the best sense of belonging, I ever felt.

"You think it'd all be different if I came out, don't you?"

"That's a start," Morgan answered, still stretching, white in the moonlight. "But it isn't about being gay or straight. It isn't about being a man. I'm not a man anymore."

I wasn't going anywhere, but he held me firmly. He was absolutely dry. The sweat on my chest was evaporating fast in the chill, my flesh was a rush of bumps. I felt my balls get tight, and my hips almost kicked into an involuntary grind against his, but my heart was still pounding, freezing me in dizziness. I still couldn't believe that Morgan, young Morgan's gorgeous arms were tying up with mine again. "It's about being alive, James. I'm alive now. Let me give you back the gift you made me believe in." He kissed me, just a brush, really, but my chill went away. Maybe that's when I felt that his lips were now hairless. And when I noticed the fangs in his mouth.

"Do you know what you can do, when you're alive, when you're in the blood, too? You can join me, burn on the uphill, fly coming down! I can still feel what it feels like to really laugh till it hurts! And when I break Three Mile Hill, like, high over the bed-ridden town, I salute them, Jim, like this—"

Morgan jumped from my arms, landing on one of the gravestones, his back arched, his arms open to the sky. "Hey, everyone who said I was a spooky freak in high school, FUCK YOU, I'M ALIVE! Hey, class of '77, FUCK YOU, I'M ALIVE!"

It only took two or three fuck-you howls and I was screaming with him, screaming my raw throat to rags. Hey, Boom-Boom, FUCK YOU, I'M ALIVE! Fleetwood Mac, FUCK! That police psychiatrist YOU! who said I wasn't competent FUCK YOU, displacing my sexual taboos I'M with a meticulous fantasy ALIVE! FUCK the whole fucking world YOUUUU! All the boys who could never take Morgan's place FUCK YOUUUUUU!!!"

I collapsed on the grass. "Just by loving a man, you put yourself outside and you loved it. Now go all the way. The price of our pleasure, James, isn't much. Just immortality. Do you remember what you told me when you showed me that you were a vampire, here, when you bled me on this spot, twenty years ago? When you initiated me?"

" 'You'll be blood of my blood,' " I answered, hoarse.

He had me in a half nelson, pushing just hard enough to burn a little, saying, "It's good that you're resisting; it heats the blood. But you must understand I'm doing this for you, James. You inspired my whole journey, and now you're coming with me."

Blood doesn't make the smoothest or the longest lasting sexual lubricant, but it is certainly the hottest. I first tried it with Morgan. It has worked for me many times since.

I was open, on my heels in the grass. I let him come. I helped Morgan rip my throat with his teeth, watched him paint his chest, his stomach, and his cock with my blood, I knew I was finally going to feel him the way he had felt me. He pointed his cock toward me and I impaled myself. I don't know if it was my imagination, but I could feel both our hearts beating inside his cock in my bloody hole. Once again, in our graveyard, we were biting and sucking, sucking and fucking each other, beating hard.

Some of you probably want to hear the blow-by-blow like a porno video—I know the police shrink did last time—but I was feeling too much to know things like that. I lost track of whose cock was whose, whose blood was whose. I didn't know where Morgan ended and I began.

And that's how I went from becoming a pretend vampire into a real one. My lover transformed me. What you have to understand is that it was a gift.

"Don't just spend one night in my veins, James," he begged me, his mouth spilling a little life, "Please...run with me. I don't ask twice."

Then we ran till we were flying, out of the graveyard, into the woods, along the river to the school. I was just hitting the practice field when I heard the sirens, saw the red lights, and noticed that Morgan was gone. He had let me win the race again, but while we were running, we were dancing, fuck you, and finally alive.

I'm cold now; besides, you know the rest. I can't stop bleeding. It's dawn, you understand, and I don't want to keep Morgan and the other children of the night waiting.

FROM THE ASSOCIATED PRESS Monday, October 11th: Belleville police apprehended a 37-year-old suspect in a twenty-year chain of unsolved cannibalistic sex crimes tonight. The suspect, James Tremblay, an unemployed Belleville man, had aroused suspicion when he acted "strangely," according to attendees of a local high school reunion. Although the suspect died in custody of self-inflicted throat wounds sustained hours before the arrest, a journal containing detailed accounts of stalking and sexual torture was found in his West Side apartment, providing the first evidence in the unsolved 1977 disappearance of Belleville High athletic star Morgan Behrman. Belleville police had no comment about Tremblay's 1991 arrest for loitering on the campus grounds. The body will be cremated October 13th.

SUPERHEROES

CAITLÍN R. KIERNAN

THE third Saturday night of July, Sunday morning now, and the air was rain cool and smelled like asphalt steam when Darby and Carter left the theater, stepped out of the artificial chill and popcorn butter stink, Pinky walking in their footsteps. The third weekend of the month and the one weekend that Classic Cinema showed *The Rocky Horror Picture Show*, one show only, midnight Saturday; this ritual as sacred to them as anything in a church had ever been, liturgy of noisemakers and squirt guns, toilet paper and melba toast sacraments.

Stingy allotment, one night of glitz and sparkle a month for a Georgia town, and the only night when hardly anyone treated them like freaks, one night when Darby and Carter could wear lipstick and eyeliner in public. And something to do besides sit in Carter's bedroom or his bedroom, listening to their music and smoking, making out sometimes and Pinky prattling on about who she thought was the cutest member of The Cure this week, or what it would be like to sleep with Trent Reznor. Their costumes and makeup a little better every time, almost as good as the college kids who stood under the screen and acted out the film, scene by scene, Darby always going as one of the Transylvanian party guests and Carter in drag as Columbia. Pinky too fat to be Magenta, too fat for the French maid outfit, but it didn't stop her, no matter how many hints they dropped and they couldn't ever just come right out and tell her.

Darby stopped just outside the theater doors, ran both hands through his black hair and a few grains of rice fell out and bounced around his feet. "You got any cigarettes left?" Carter asked him and he fished the half-empty pack of Camels from the inside pocket of his tuxedo jacket, gave one to Carter, one to Pinky even though she was always bumming smokes, never had any to offer anyone else. And they stood watching the crowd as it squeezed through the doors and broke apart in the parking lot, at least half in costume, slackers and punks and townies, University students and a surly clump of frat boy lookie-looks. Some of the live cast came out and the girl that played Columbia, dead ringer for Little Nell, stopped and smiled wide at Carter.

"Nice outfit," she said and "Thanks," he replied and then she smiled even wider. "Shit, I thought you were a real girl," and she laughed, skipped away to catch up with the others. "Bitch," Pinky said, sneered after the girl. And Carter just shrugged, "It's a sort of a compliment," he said.

Quick *clack, clack, clack* on the concrete for them and a half spin, not real taps but beer bottle caps stuck to the soles of his shoes, tipped his gold-sequined top hat and the tails of his gold-sequined jacket flying out behind. Someone clapped for him and it got a half-smile from Darby, hard not to smile for Carter.

"Are we gonna go back to your house, Darby? " Pinky asked, and then, whispered, like the world's biggest secret, like something dangerous, "I got three Darvon out of my mother's medicine cabinet this morning."

Darby looked across the parking lot, past the piss-yellowy pools of light and the cars lined up in front of the theater, the people getting in and driving away and he squinted, as if trying to see further. "Look, Pinky, can you get another ride home tonight?" and he knew that she could, at least three or four others still hanging around the doors she could beg a ride off easy if she tried, or he wouldn't have asked.

"Sure, I guess I could," she said, "if you guys have other plans," sounding more hurt than she was and Darby groaned inside, not even half up to Pinky's calculated self-pity tonight, not up to his own guilt, as involuntary as gagging. And Carter watching him, Cleopatra-eyes full of doubt, misgiving, and he knew Carter was hoping that he'd change his mind at the last minute, after all.

"Yeah, we do, kinda," he said, instead. "But I'll call you tomorrow, okay?"

Big Pinky frown, dramatic loud sigh. "That's okay," she said, dumpier, white-faced Eeyore, "I'll find a ride. But I'll hold on to the pills. Maybe tomorrow night?" and "Yeah," Darby said. "Maybe. We'll call you." And she hugged them both and walked away, trailing her own private cloud of cigarette smoke and dejection and patchouli fumes.

"You're being mean to her again," Carter said and Darby looked back out at the parking lot. Fewer people now, easier to see all the way across. "Bullshit," he said and pushed his sunglasses down toward the tip of his nose, stared at Carter over the rims. "Look, you promised you'd do this with me. You didn't have to promise. If you'd rather be popping pain-killers with a fag hag, that's your business." Words he knew would cut, would find their mark.

"Jesus, Darby. That's what I mean. There's no point talking about her like that. I said I'd fucking come."

Deep drag off his Camel and Darby flicked the butt into the gutter, started walking and he knew that Carter would follow, immediately heard the clack, clack, clack of his Columbia shoes on the blacktop. And he stopped so Carter could catch up. "Can't we at least go and change our clothes first?" and more sharply than was necessary, "There isn't time," too sharp but the adrenaline was getting to him. "We have to be there at exactly 2:30. Exactly 2:30, Carter. He won't wait around if we're not."

And Carter followed him, silent except for his shoes, past the dark-ened A&P, the Chevron station closed up for the night and the row of dumpsters a little further back, farthest edge of the parking lot from the theater, where the asphalt ended in sticky red mud and pine trees, pothole alley behind the shopping center. Much darker back there, tree shadows, whispering needles and dumpster shadows, wet garbage stink. The quar-ter moon slipped in and out of the clouds, too small and too cold and much too far away to be a comfort.

Darby looked at his wristwatch, tilted its face back toward the shop-ping center glow to read the dial.

"Then, if he doesn't come by 2:35, we can go?"

"He's coming," Darby said, final word, and Carter held his hand tight and they waited.

A RUMOR passed between the dark children and their computer screens, wishful thought gathering substance and momentum like a phos-phor snowball as they passed their electronic notes around the world. Veiled hints and insinuation hidden between goth band gossip and love letters to vampires, fishnet need and black vinyl desire. Something that might have been real all along or a collective wet dream they'd forced into a deal with reality, or something else altogether.

And it had been seven months since Darby found that first mention of Jimmy DeSade on alt.gothic, rainy January and the three of them at Carter's house that night. Getting fucked up on Robitussin and Pinky hogging the stereo, playing the same Daisy Chainsaw CD over and over again while Darby and Carter sat at Carter's new Compaq Presario, blue-white monitor glare competing with the candlelight. That first message, hardly a whisper, ...*about as real as Jimmy DeSade, Shelley, dear. Get thee a fucking clue.* Prickle sick rush of excitement in Darby's stomach, then, inexplicable, but the same rising-sinking prickle as the first time Carter had offered to suck him off, and he'd followed that thread back as far as it went, *Re: Are Cheetos gothick?! (Was: Poseur Alert from Brooklyn)*, followed the original thread and that was the only time the name came up. A simile, nothing more, but he'd scanned through every other message in the newsgroup anyway, stayed at the keyboard long after Carter had lost interest and gone off to talk Pinky into playing something else.

And when he hadn't found anything, had posted *Who's Jimmy DeSade?* and just four words to the message, *Well? Who is he?* No reply that night, no answer for days afterwards, bleak slate skies and that name in his head, and Carter had started to complain about all the time he spent online. "My parents are gonna absolutely shit a cat when they get the AOL bill, Darby," and when he was about to turn loose, forget it, another mention, *Like the junk heap Jimmy DeSade drives, right?* and that time he'd e-mailed the poster who'd written the message, Salome@omniserv.com and the response had said only, *shhhhhhhh and Listen, babygoth...* Those words read over and over until he had a hard-on, and he'd written back, *Listen for what?! (And don't call me a babygoth, I'm 16)*, but there had never been an answer. And he'd found himself imagining, fantasizing Jimmy DeSade, making pretty pictures, awful pictures, in his head whenever he and Carter fucked around. A rattletrap car and the man behind the wheel, big scarecrow man and his face always lost in the thinner bits of the fantasy, but that car clear enough, bumping down a dark and dirt-paved road, the choking dust trailing out behind.

"I'M cold," Carter said, standing as close to Darby as he could. Thunder not far away, toward Normaltown or Bogart and for the last five minutes a misting rain. They'd stepped back, a little shelter in the cover of the pines, wet needles crunching like soggy breakfast cereal under their shoes.

"Stop whining," Darby said and he didn't take his eyes off the road, just an alley, really, running between the woods and the rear of the shopping center.

"Fuck you, Darby. It's raining and I'm cold."

"Go home, then," more a threat than an alternative, and Carter stepped back, one foot or two, and "I feel like Charlie Brown in drag, waiting with Linus for the stupid fucking Great Pumpkin, Darby. That's what this is like. Waiting for the goddamn Great Pumpkin."

"Then go home, Carter. I'm not forcing you to do anything and I'm tired of your whining."

Instead, "What time is it?" Carter asked him and Darby didn't want to look at his watch, didn't want to know how fast the minutes were creeping by, adding up, making a fool of him. "It's not time yet," he said.

And he took out the razor blade, the one he always kept with him now, stainless steel in his pocket since the first night he'd talked Carter into letting him cut and press his eager lips to the open wound. Catch the warmth, the warmth that spilled out into the world, into him, like light. Fingered it nervously like a coin or a good luck charm.

"What do you want?" Carter said, looking at the razor the nervous way he always looked at it.

"I just want to know," Darby said. "If he's real, I just want to know."

"IS it gonna hurt?" Carter had asked the night in February, first-time night. Thunderstorm night and Darby had bought the pack of Schick blades at the drug store that afternoon, when there had only been prologue black clouds building over the town and wind that smelled like spring.

"No," he'd said, not knowing but by then his dick so hard it hurt and when he closed his eyes he saw Jimmy DeSade coming, rolling along back roads and empty midnight interstate. Wanting to care if he hurt Carter but not caring, anyway. Not caring about anything but the way it would feel when the blade traced a paper cut line along Carter's shoulder, dividing cream skin, tear here, dotted line; not caring about anything but the face he couldn't see behind the dirty windshield.

Raging hard-on for a hearsay, gossip phantom or just a game the netgeeks hadn't let him in on; butt of their jokes, the way he'd begged for details and every now and then a scrap or a crumb thrown his way or not hidden before he found it, just enough that he wouldn't forget and never any more. Ligeia@well.com and a signature line, *The children of the night can't sing for shit*—Jimmy DeSade. Or, taunting, infuriating uncertainty just for him: Nitejaw1@perfidia.co.uk and *...those lousy wankers haven't put out any new songs worth shit since Jimmy D. and Salmagundi were a thing.*

And Carter had only flinched, the cut an inch long but longer than he'd meant, deeper, the thick blood welling like spilled ink in the candlelight and his heart skipping hard beats by the time he'd kissed it away. Soft moans from Carter that had only made him harder and when Darby had reached around Carter's waist, he'd been hard, too.

Outside the rain had turned to hail and the thunder had sounded like judgment rattling at the windows.

"JUST admit it, Carter. Admit you're scared and go the hell home while there's still time."

"Why won't you tell me what time it is, Darby? That's all I asked. If you're right, what's the big deal?"

But Darby kept his wrist where Carter couldn't see, where he wouldn't have to watch the hour hand and minute hand, rushing second hand; 2:38 last time he'd risked a glance and he hadn't even told Carter that. It was raining harder now, steady drizzle and then coming straight down and they were both getting soaked, makeup running and both of them shivering soppy inside their costumes. Although Darby tried hard not to shiver, tried to reveal no sign of discomfort, to show no hint the cold was getting in, that he was anything but confident.

"I should leave you here, Darby. You'd have it coming, after the way you talked to Pinky. After the way you've been talking to me."

"Just shut up, Carter."

"You see what I mean? I really should leave you standing here alone in the fucking rain all night."

And Darby took something from the inside of his tux jacket, the rain soaked through and the paper wet, wet page from Carter's printer and he read the words there again. At least the ink hadn't started to run or smear and it was all still there, still real.

"Just leave your snotty ass standing out here to get the flu or pneumonia. Christ, Darby, the rain is going to ruin my costume..."

And Darby turned on him, all the ripe and rotten frustration getting out through his eyes, green fire ringed with smeared mascara and the razor clenched between his thumb and index finger. "GO THE FUCK HOME, CARTER! NOW, GODDAMN IT!" and Carter just stood there, staring at him, disbelief and his scared face like a ruined watercolor. A big run in his hose from their scramble up the low and muddy bank to the shelter of the pines and he'd gotten tangled in some briars.

"If you can't shut up and stand there a few goddamn minutes without whining, I don't want you here."

Lower lip trembling and a tear distinct from the rain on Carter's cheeks, the kind of sniveling shit Pinky would pull and Darby pushed him so hard he almost slipped and fell.

"He is coming," the soggy printout held so Carter could see. "I didn't make this up. I didn't imagine this."

"No, but maybe you're being too stupid to know someone's just playing a joke on you," and Darby gritted his teeth, swung the razor blade and fabric *shrrriped* when it caught the lapels of Carter's jacket, wide gash through the dripping sequins and the fabric underneath.

"You crazy son of a bitch," and that was all before Carter was running, *clack, clack, clack, clack* across the wet road; Darby looked down at his hand, traitorous, alien thing at the end of his arm and the wet glint of the razor there. Looked across the road and Carter had stopped on the other side, stood with his back to concrete walls painted the latex color of oatmeal, no shelter at all from the rain over there, but he stood very still and stared back at Darby.

"Jesus, Carter," rain muffled words and *I'm sorry,* but just inside his head, because he was afraid it wouldn't matter, too late or just that Carter wouldn't hear. So he went back to waiting, and Carter waited with him, or apart from him, on the other side.

APRIL and Darby had been failing algebra again, his parents talking about summer school like it was the boogeyman and bitching about his hair, that he'd started wearing eyeliner to school. And *It's no fucking wonder you're always getting your ass kicked,* said his father. And *Other boys your age have started dating,* said his mother. He'd taken blood from Carter's shoulder every chance he got, his lips to the breach and his hand around his penis, the warm salt penny chocolate taste and orgasm, the stain on his lips and cum on the sheets of their beds. The scars and fresher cuts lined up neat on Carter's shoulder and thighs, marks a prisoner might make on the wall of his cell.

And Carter refusing to take from him, no complaints, no resistance, but no reciprocation, either. "I just don't want to, that's all."

Sitting at Carter's computer when he could and finding next to nothing, when nothing might have been a blessing, better than the teasing bits and whispers he found instead.

Balzac45@angeleno.com and *That soundz like something Jimmy DeSade would have done—before the riotz—IMHo.* No one ever answering his questions straight, when they bothered to answer them at all.

And one night, middle of the month and his bedroom window open, cricket and cicada racket underneath This Mortal Coil and Pinky had been whining, bored Pinky whine and how she wished they had fake IDs and then they could get into a club or a bar, like there was anywhere in town worth sneaking into. Atlanta, then, she'd said, Atlanta has real clubs, but only Carter had a car and his parents wouldn't ever let him drive that far. "You want to try something new, Pinky?" and Carter had looked at him, concern, confusion, and Darby had gone to the shelf where he kept his razor blades, hidden in the middle of a stack of comics and *Fangoria*, someplace his mother wouldn't look.

"Like what? A new drug?" she'd said and Carter hadn't said anything, just that look, *Are you sure, Darby? This might not be such a good idea.* And maybe betrayal, too, because hadn't he told Carter it was sex, enough like sex, even better than sex, maybe?

"No, it's not a drug. It's something else," and he'd shone her the silver and blue plastic dispenser of razor blades. "It's something different."

"Oh," she'd said. "You mean bloodletting, Darby? I've done that, with Jackie and her cousin, last year. She had a special little knife from India," and "Aren't you worried about getting AIDS?" before Carter had taken the dispenser from his open hand. "She doesn't want to do it," he'd said.

"She didn't say that, did you, Pinky?"

And she'd looked down at Carter's hand, fist squeezed tight around the blades, had shrugged, dim apprehension in her piggy eyes but she wasn't afraid and it had pissed Darby off. "Never fucking mind," and he'd taken the razor blades away from Carter, put them back safe between magazine slick covers.

"I'M sorry, Darby," shouted across the road, Carter's words getting to him through the downpour tattoo. "I am. I'm sorry." No reply, nothing he could have said, and he tried not to look at his watch, the wet crystal and hands like school yard bullies. But he did. 2:57 and he couldn't pretend it was fast, not that fast, anyway. Had checked it three times that afternoon against the time on The Weather Channel.

"Can I come back over there and stand with you, Darby?"

Lightning and thunder right away so he could make like he hadn't heard, wished he hadn't seen Carter so stark in the half-second flash of daylight. Rusty streaks of the temporary orange color he'd put in his hair running down his cheeks, hair plastered, the puddle around his heels.

"I won't say anything else, Darby. I'll keep my mouth shut."

Darby was still holding the razor, stainless steel washed clean by the rain and he didn't answer, imagined that he hadn't only cut Carter's jacket, had cut his throat and let all that blood out at once. Scalding, stickydark jet in time to Carter's heart, dark spray across the wet pine straw, bright and fading surprise and terror in Carter's eyes before he fell, sank slow-mo into Darby's waiting arms, Darby's waiting lips. Maybe that would have been enough, that one indelible act, offering, forfeiture, and maybe he wouldn't be standing here, afraid of his wristwatch. Carter yelling at him from behind the A&P. Maybe he hadn't understood, had done something wrong. Their ridiculous *Rocky Horror* clothes maybe, or that he hadn't come alone.

"Go home, Carter!" he screamed, "I don't want you here," and Carter shook his head and stood there in the rain.

IN May he'd had the dream, the only time, third Saturday of the month and so there'd been *Rocky* with Carter and Pinky and whatever they'd found to do afterwards. No sleep until almost dawn and Pinky had given him a Xanax she'd stolen from her older sister so he'd passed out cold. And standing on the long, dirt road under a swollen sun the color of a cardinal's feathers, heavy summer heat and sweat in his eyes as he watched the dust cloud coming toward him down the clay red slash between the pines. Smell of turpentine and baking air, and the sun glinting mean off the hood of the old Lincoln. Hot, rustling breeze through the needles and the wild animal sound of the car's engine, the sound of bald tires on the road and he stepped back, stood waiting in oven shade until the car rumbled to a stop, dust cloud catching up with it and sifting down around him. And the door, opening wide so the cool air washed out, wrapped itself around his ankles, slithered up the legs of his jeans. Asking him in, sanctuary (*never mind the smell, it grows on you, after a while*), refuge from the demon sun and this fucking town and his fucking parents. The hand before it retreated into air-conditioned shadows, bulky silver rings on every finger, nails like a mechanic's, oil grunge beneath those nails, except the one on his little finger, so long and sharp and gleaming perfect crimson.

"What you waitin' for, little boy?" Jimmy DeSade said, sexy smooth Brit accent and the cold air worked its way through Darby's underwear, coiled tight around his dick. "You only get asked one time."

The cold, like a dead and loving tongue and then the orgasm had awakened him, and Darby had lain in bed an hour longer, semen scabbing on his skin, staring at the afternoon sunlight through the curtains.

"PLEASE, Darby. I'm freezing."

3:19, last time he looked at his watch before he'd taken it off and thrown it across the road at Carter. Faint smash when it hit the back wall of the grocery store instead, and Carter had picked up what was left.

"Let's just go back to my house," he said, easy to hear him now because the rain had stopped. Dripped down around him from the limbs, from his hair and clothes. Dripped as loud and constant as the watch had ticked. "I'm gonna *have* to go soon, Darby, and I don't want to leave you out here by yourself."

"Go on, then," Darby said. "Run away home."

He stood out of sight, under the trees, had sliced the tip end of every finger with the razor blade, cut broad X's on the backs of both hands and smeared his face with the blood, tasted it, his own blood for once. And it tasted and felt no different in his mouth than Carter's, but meant nothing, except that he was bleeding.

"Please come home with me."

And Darby turned and walked deeper into the woods, briars and brambles tearing at his black clothes, his shoes sinking in pine straw mud and before long he couldn't hear Carter calling him anymore.

"IT totally changes the whole movie," Pinky had said, muggy June night, still a week before *Rocky Horror* and Carter had rented the video so they could practice the responses. Then back to his bedroom, Pinky and Carter talking while Darby sat at the computer. "It's the song that shows us how Brad and Janet have been changed by everything that happened to them in the castle," she'd said, "And when it's not there, it changes everything."

"Well, I've called the theater three or four times now," Carter said, "and asked them to *please* get the British release instead, but I don't think they're ever gonna. They *always* show the British print in Atlanta."

And Darby had typed in Carter's password and waited, wait that always seemed like a short forever while the modem dialed into the server and Pinky and Carter's conversation nothing but annoying. "You've got mail," and he'd clicked the mailbox, just one letter waiting, 101017.865@compuserve.com, and the subject line, one word, DeSade. And his heart had skipped and hammered.

"The verse Janet sings. That's how you know it's really a vampire story," Pinky said, "and that all the Frankenstein stuff is just superficial."

Even though Darby had stopped asking questions in April, had given up and he'd almost called Carter to come, to see, before he moved the mouse, the pointer, and double-clicked again.

"And that's why Brad and Janet are so fucked up in Shock Treatment, because it's really making fun of all those old science fiction movies where everything gets like magically okay and normal again as soon as the monster's gone."

The message so short, lean and ribsy sentences, rationed words, and he'd read it over and over again: ...an associate of Mr. DeSade... and He finds this perseverance endearing... and, then, ...meeting might be arranged, if you're interested... Yours Sincerely, V. and Darby had told the computer to print, stared unblinking at the bright screen while the noisy dot-matrix printer put ink to paper, making it solid, substantial, before he'd moved the pointer over to the reply icon.

"Loss of innocence," Pinky had said, "and the illusion of morality. Nothing can ever be the same again. That's what 'Superheroes' is saying at the end of the movie," sounding pleased with herself, and then the wail of a train whistle through the open window, far away and coming closer.

AND he moved faster and faster between the trees, caught his feet in creeper vines and deadfall tangles, fell and got up and kept moving, running finally. No thought to where, except that his feet would carry him away from Carter and his own shitty life, away from the town and school, away from everything. A small creek strangling with the night's runoff and he lost a shoe on the silty bottom, pulled the other off, full of mud and water anyway, flung it away into the dark and ran on in his sock feet. Sharp, jabbing sticks and rocks bruising his feet until the pain from the cuts on his hands seemed unimportant.

And the trees ended, all at once and the narrow cleft of a dirt road before they began again. Began again to go on that way forever, and Darby heard the rattle and grind of the car's old engine, death rattle, oil-dry grind, before he saw the headlights. Nothing but the headlights, set far apart like reptile eyes or the space between him and morning. Moving so fast, bouncing over ruts and potholes, bearing down and Darby waited in the trees, breathless, side stitch and feet bleeding through his socks. Until the car was almost on him, and he stepped across.

LETTING GO

EDO VAN BELKOM

I don't want to trickle out. I want to pour till the pail is empty, the last bit going out in a gush, not drops.
—EMILY CARR

CHRIS Geary hurried down the hall, checking the faces of those he passed in search of one that was familiar.

A few more steps and he found who he'd been looking for. "Why haven't you released him yet?" he said, sounding more demanding than inquisitive. "Why haven't you sent him home?"

Doctor Sheldon Katz looked up and down the hallway, then led Chris over to a quiet corner. There, he pressed his lips together, shook his head, and said, "Because he doesn't *want* to go home."

Chris fell silent as the shock of the words settled in. He and Glen had been partners for over eight years and were as close as any two people could be. Wanting to stay in the hospital wasn't like Glen.

Sure, Glen had been the more adventurous of the two—he had been the one to suggest separate vacations, after all—but no matter where he went or for how long, he'd always looked forward to coming home. So why on earth would he want to spend his last days in the cold and impersonal surroundings of a hospital when he could be at home, surrounded by people who loved him and who would care for him to the end?

It didn't make any sense.

"I don't believe that," Chris said at last. "He should be home. You said so yourself, last night."

"I know I did," said the doctor. "But we had another patient die in the night, a patient in the same room as Glen."

"Mark?"

The doctor nodded. "And when I asked Glen this morning if he wanted to check out of the hospital, to go home, he said no. He said he wanted to stay here like Mark...wanted to die here like Mark."

Chris shook his head again. "But that's not right. He should be home with me."

"I agree," said the doctor, "but we can't ship him out against his wishes. He *wants* to remain in the hospital so we have to respect that, just like we have to respect his wish that we not give him anything more for his pain."

"What?"

The doctor dragged his fingertips across his forehead. Clearly this whole situation had been causing him some grief. "So far he's refused morphine, Percodan, and most of the other pain medications we've offered. All he's allowed us to give him is a few Tylenol Threes, and not many of those, either."

"But that's crazy!" Chris had watched plenty of his friends die from AIDS these past few years. Although in its final stages the disease could claim lives quickly, the actual death always seemed to take forever, biding its time for days while its victim suffered long, agonizing hours full of excruciating pain.

"I know, I know," said the doctor, his tone suggesting he'd already given up trying to apply rational thought to this case. "But that's not the half of it. The reason he doesn't want any medication is because he says there's something coming for him—the same something that took Mark—and he wants to be ready for it when it does."

The words cut straight to Chris's heart. He closed his eyes and leaned heavily against the wall to steady himself. Then, after a few moments, he took a deep breath and said, "Obviously, he's not thinking clearly." Another deep breath, and a sigh. "Let me sign something, a paper putting him into my care. I'll take him home, I'll take care of—"

The doctor shook his head. "Even though HIV can damage the central nervous system, our specialists haven't been able to detect any significant intellectual or psychological dysfunction in Glen."

Chris laughed under his breath. "So, you're saying that just because he's talking crazy, it doesn't mean that he is."

The doctor shrugged. "Basically."

"And you expect me to believe that?"

"Look, Mister—" The doctor hesitated.

"Geary. Chris Geary."

"Look, Mr. Geary, instead of you arguing about it with me, why don't you just go and talk it over with him yourself. Wouldn't that be best?"

Chris stood there trying to think of something more to say. The doctor was right, he should be talking about this with Glen, but it was somehow easier to argue with a stranger, even a doctor, than face Glen on his deathbed.

At last he took a deep breath, and consigned himself to it. "All right, then," he said. "Maybe I'll do that."

THE room's smell was a familiar one to Chris.

It smelled like Death.

No matter how many friends he'd seen die this way, he could never get used to it. How could he? How could he get used to seeing someone he knew and remembered as a beautiful and vibrant human being cruelly diminished to something transient—still not finished living, but yet to be embraced by death. And even if he had become used to it by now, become numbed by it all, would it have prepared him for it happening to Glen?

No, nothing could have done that.

Chris stepped silently toward the bed on the right side of the room. Glen was asleep with the sheets pulled up to his neck, one arm on top of the sheets, one arm beneath.

Although Chris had been here just yesterday, he was somewhat shocked by Glen's condition. It seemed to have deteriorated drastically overnight. The skin on his neck, face, and arm were covered by new and bigger tumors and lesions. And the parts of his flesh that hadn't been overrun by Kaposi's sarcoma were now affected by rashes and patches of eczema. Some of his hair had fallen out, and the newly-exposed patches of scalp were the same pale white color as the rest of him. There was an IV running into his exposed arm, but it was a just a token attempt to keep his body nourished after the thrush in his mouth and esophagus had made eating virtually impossible.

Chris took a seat by the bed and sat down. He continued to look at Glen, finding it hard to believe that this was the same man he'd loved for so many years.

Just a year ago Glen had weighed a hundred and ninety-five pounds, worked out daily, and had a body that an aerobics instructor might envy. Now he was half that weight, shriveled and emaciated as if his life-force had been sucked from his body, leaving behind little more than an empty husk and a life's worth of memories.

Glen's eyes slowly came open.

"Hi, guy!" said Chris, doing his best to smile.

Glen looked over at Chris, then closed his eyes. After a couple of breaths, his lips began to move.

Chris got up and brought his head close to Glen's mouth.

"I'm still here," Glen whispered.

Chris couldn't be sure if the words were meant to be a question or a statement. "Yes, you are," he said, "but..."

Glen's eyes opened again.

"But I'd like to take you home with me. You'd be more comfortable there and—"

"No," said Glen, his voice stronger than before. "I have to wait for him."

Chris was caught a little off-guard by this, but managed to recover quickly enough. "You could wait for him at home," he said. "We could wait for him together."

"He won't find me there." The words came more quickly and were edged with a strange sort of excitement that forced Glen to pause to catch his breath. "I have to wait for him...here."

"Who? Wait for who?"

"Death."

Chris felt his stomach turn and his knees go weak. It was obvious that dementia had set in and Glen was no longer in control of his mind. If he could see that, surely the doctor—any doctor—could see it too.

"He came for Mark last night," Glen went on, mumbling the words. "And he's coming back for me."

Chris looked over at the empty bed on the other side of the room, and felt tears beginning to well up behind his eyes. He rubbed a sleeve across his brow and took a deep breath. "Why don't you at least let the doctors give you some medicine...just for the pain."

"No!" said Glen in what sounded like his normal speaking voice. "I have to be ready for him. I want to feel his hands on me, touching me..." Glen's voice faded and he drifted off to sleep.

Chris just shook his head.

Glen had always been the stronger of the two, both physically and emotionally. He was the rock, the pillar of the relationship, the one who had always been best at handling life's problems. And now he was being the same way in death, being strong, handling it as if it were just another problem.

Maybe he was being too strong.

And then all at once it hit Chris like a punch in the gut, the hard realization that he wasn't so much afraid for Glen as he was for himself. When his time came, when his grasp on life began slipping, Glen would be gone and he would have to face it alone.

That's what scared him most, dying a long, lonely death.

He reached over and held Glen's hand. The bony fingers curled around his, holding them weakly for a long, long time.

A few hours later a nurse came in to check on Glen. She was a middle-aged black woman, large around the middle with strong arms and legs, and a face that seemed impassive and impervious to the dying that went on around her.

She took Glen's temperature and blood pressure as if they really mattered and then fluffed his pillow in an attempt to make him comfortable.

Then she knelt down beneath the bed and unhooked Glen's urine bag from where it hung.

Chris looked away as she took the bag over to the bathroom and poured its contents into the toilet.

When she returned to Glen's bedside, the nurse stopped to look at Chris. "Are you staying the night?" she said flatly.

"Pardon me?"

"You can stay the night if you want." She pointed at the empty bed on the other side of the room. "I can make it up for you, if you like."

Chris hesitated a moment, his first thought being that a man had died in that bed the night before. It gave him the creeps, but he realized it was a way in which he could stay with Glen through the night... his last night, most likely.

"Yes," he said. "That would be wonderful. Thank you very much."

She smiled at him then, a sympathetic and understanding sort of smile that made Chris think she knew more about what he was going through than she let on. "No problem," she said. "It's important that you be here... For him."

Hearing that made Chris feel a little better, even though it sounded as if she'd added that last part to clarify who would be benefiting from his staying the night.

"He needs me to be with him," Chris nodded.

She just smiled at him. "Right."

Over the next half hour, the nurse came and went bringing sheets and pillows and blankets, and by nightfall the bed was ready. "I brought you some extra blankets," she said, piling up the folded blankets on the end of the bed. "He likes having the window left open through the night."

Chris looked at her strangely.

"I know," the nurse said with a shrug. "Summer's over and the nights are getting cold, but he insists we keep the window open. Mr. Cevert did too."

"Mark?"

The nurse nodded, then sighed. "Anyway, you have a nice night, now. I'll see you in the morning."

"Good night," said Chris, waving to the nurse but looking at the open window. It was another thing that didn't make sense. Glen never slept with the window open, especially in the colder months.

He must really want to die, thought Chris. Why else would he want an open window in October when the chill of the night would only help to quicken his demise?

The thought sent a shiver down Chris' spine. When it passed, he slumped back in his chair, cradled his head in his hands and began to cry.

CHRIS awoke some time later, stiff and cold.

The room was bathed in the soft glow of moonlight, the window frames and cross-pieces slicing it up into pieces of light and shadow that covered the floor like the bars of a prison cell. All except for the open window. There the light shone through unbroken, leaving a solid square of light on the floor like a doorway to somewhere else.

The open window had also caused the temperature in the room to fall into the mid-sixties and Chris' bones had begun to ache from it. As he stretched his arms and legs to get his blood circulating, he wondered what kind of effect the cold was having on Glen.

He got up, leaned over the bed and checked. Glen was resting, his breathing deep and regular and edged every so often by a long moan of pain.

Every time he moaned, Chris reflexively searched Glen's body for some thorn poking into his side, looking for something tangible he could remove to ease the pain. But of course, there was nothing there, and he had to remind himself that there was nothing he could do for him.

Chris pulled the sheets up to Glen's chin, then stood there watching him sleep. As the minutes passed, Chris began to grow tired and considered sitting back down in the chair, but doubted he could get comfortable in it again after so many hours. And so, for the first time that night, the bed on the other side of room began to look inviting. He decided to use it, catch a few hour's rest, then return to the chair—to Glen's bedside—before morning.

He walked across the room and stopped at the open window. For a moment he considered closing it, but he knew doing so would probably awaken Glen, not to mention upset him. As a compromise, he found the room thermostat and turned it up to seventy-five. Hopefully, it would all even out.

On the other side of the room, Chris slipped off his shoes and crawled into bed still dressed in his clothes.

The bed felt cold.

He pulled a couple of blankets over him, but still he felt chilled. He told himself it was just the temperature in the room, and had nothing to do with a man dying in the bed the night before. But the thought continued to tumble through his mind, over and over again, until it was finally—mercifully—shrouded by the heavy curtain of sleep.

And at last he lay still.

CHRIS was awakened by the feeling of pressure on his throat, the warm press of something that was both sharp and wet.

When the pressure was relieved, he tried to open his eyes. His eyelids were incredibly heavy and it seemed to take forever for him to raise them. When his eyes were finally open, his vision was clouded by a reddish sort of haze that prevented him from seeing much in the shadow-darkened room.

But he was determined to have a look around. He tried to lift his head, but a sharp pain in his neck forced him to drop his head back onto the pillow. Unable to move now, he rolled his eyes until they were pointed down and he was looking over his body and across the room at Glen's bed.

It was hard to distinguish much detail through the haze, but there seemed to be someone—not a doctor or nurse—leaning over Glen, slowly pulling back the sheets and removing his catheter.

The figure was roughly human in shape—a man perhaps—and dressed completely in black, as if clothed by the night itself. After it had pulled back Glen's sheets, it seemed to rear back and open its mouth as if in a smile.

And then...

And then something glinted in the moonlight, something sharp and deadly like the edge of a blade, or the point of a knife.

Chris opened his mouth to scream.

No!

But no sound escaped his lips.

He was just too weak.

All he could do was move his eyes.

All he could do was watch.

And so, while a new and still colder wind blew in through the open window, Chris watched.

The black-clad figure's bare hands were on Glen's body, touching him all over. Initially Glen had stirred, moaned as he usually did when struck by a particularly sharp stab of pain. But as the figure continued to run his hand's over Glen's body, the sounds Glen made began to soften.

They began to sound like moans of pleasure.

For a moment Chris closed his eyes and listened. He could almost picture he and Glen alone together, making love.

The longer he listened, the more real it all seemed.

The hospital and the disease and the loneliness all began to fade, seeming to become a nightmare that might simply vanish upon waking.

But then he heard Glen speak. The words were unintelligible, but the sound of his voice was unmistakable.

Chris opened his eyes.

And the reality came rushing back to him, harder and colder then ever.

Glen was dying.

And there was nothing he could do about it.

Or was there?

For the first time in minutes, Chris could wiggle his toes. He tried his hands and found that his fingers moved now too.

In a few more minutes, he'd be able to move his arms and legs. With a sense of urgency, he began to clench and unclench his fists beneath the blankets, hoping it would help to get his blood flowing again.

It was working.

He was able to see a little clearer now, even though what he was seeing didn't make much sense.

He couldn't be sure, but it looked as if Glen had an erection. That was impossible, Chris thought. Glen's sex drive had been parked for months as his body had concentrated on more important matters—like surviving.

But there it was, a hard-on.

The dark man moved closer to it.

Chris opened his mouth to scream.

"No!" he cried.

The sound of his voice stopped the dark man from doing anything more. He looked over at Chris.

He could move his arms and legs now, but just barely. He threw down the blankets and struggled to climb out of the bed.

The dark man watched Chris for a moment, then turned his attention back to Glen.

Chris was utterly exhausted, his body feeling ten times heavier than normal. It was a struggle just to set his feet on the floor.

But somehow he managed.

He headed across the room.

The dark man was still hunched over Glen's body, his lips about to encircle the head of Glen's penis.

"Stop it!" Chris shouted.

And for the second time, the sound of Chris's voice halted the dark man's movements.

Chris made it to the edge of Glen's bed, and waved his arm at the dark man in an attempt to push him away.

But in mid-swing the dark man's left hand shot up, catching Chris's arm at the wrist and holding it there, immobile. Chris fought to wrench himself free but his body was far too weak to put up much of a fight. Yet, he continued to struggle, to stop this monster from—

"Let go!" said a voice.

It was Glen's voice. At the sound of it, Chris stopped struggling and the dark man's grip lessened slightly.

"Let go!" Glen repeated.

The dark man released his hold on Chris as if he were following Glen's command. Funny thing was, Chris wasn't so sure Glen had been talking to the dark man.

And so Chris just stood by and watched as the dark man's lips pulled back, exposing two needle-sharp incisors. He pressed them against Glen's taut flesh, gently at first, then harder and harder.

The points pierced the skin, and the fangs sank deep.

Glen gasped, then let out a long, drawn-out moan. It was a deep and guttural sound, indicative of his first true pleasure in months.

The dark man sucked at the wound, not stopping until Glen's body began to spasm, shuddering hard as life flowed out, and death flowed in.

And then Glen lay still, the room eerily silent except for the cold wind blowing in through the open window.

The dark man rose up, pausing a moment before pulling the sheets up over Glen's body. At last, he turned toward Chris.

And for a moment their eyes made contact. The dark man's icy stare was strikingly intense, forcing Chris to close his eyes to break their hold on him.

It was a long time before he opened them again.

"MISTER?"

The voice was familiar.

"Mister, are you okay?"

Chris opened his eyes. He was back on the bed. In front of him was a nurse, the same one as yesterday.

But yesterday she had smiled. Today, she looked sad, maybe even a little worried.

And all at once he knew.

He pushed back the blankets and tried to get out of the bed, but his legs and arms were weak and stiff and sore. He tried again, moving more slowly, and with the nurse's help was able to stand.

On the other side of the room, there were orderlies and nurses around Glen's bed. They had masks on and gloves and...

"Wait!"

Chris hobbled across the room, each step bringing life back to his cold-stiffened joints.

He approached the bed slowly, his eyes closed until his hand touched the foot of the bed. Then he opened his eyes.

Glen was dead, that was obvious.

And then a sense of relief washed over Chris, not so much because Glen's suffering was over, but because of the look on Glen's face.

It was a look Chris hadn't seen in months.

He was smiling, truly happy.

Looking at that smile, Chris didn't fear the future anymore. He would be strong.

And when the end came, he would not run from Death.

Instead, he would embrace it...

Like a lover.

THE DEAD OF WINTER

MICHAEL ROWE

For the Original Six Algonquin Posse

"**THAT** guy's out there again," Juicy whispered to Vinnie. "I bet he's waitin' for you to bring him out his dinner. You know who I mean," she giggled. "That guy who always asks for extra tomatoes with his chicken, and drinks his coffee ice cold. The writer-guy. You know," she giggled again, elbowing Vinnie in the side. "That queer."

"Oh, and *you* know he's a queer," Vinnie said irritably, loading Juicy's tray with the dinner he had just prepared. The restaurant was almost empty tonight, probably because of the snow. The radio said it was going to be a blizzard. Vinnie wished the blizzard would hurry up so he could go home early instead of dealing with this dumb bitch Juicy. "You're one hundred percent sure he's a queer, just because he don't have a girlfriend. *That you've seen*," Vinnie added significantly.

"He never comes in here with nobody," insisted Juicy. "And he just moved here. He lives in that old red house on Martin Street. Mrs. Winfield's old house. He lives with a guy he says is his cousin. Why would *anybody* move here, never mind with their cousin? Anyway, he's way past old enough to be married, and I think he's rich."

"Maybe he just *wanted* to move here," Vinnie said defensively. He felt oddly protective of the writer-guy. The writer-guy seemed nice, minded his own business. And he appeared to appreciate Vinnie's cooking, at least Juicy said he did. "Though why *anyone* would move here if they didn't have to is something *I* don't understand. And maybe he *likes* living with his cousin. You watch too much *Melrose Place*, Juicy. You think everything's a fuckin' soap opera."

"Cousin? Yeah, right," Juicy sneered. "*Kissin'* cousins, maybe. He's either a queer, or he sells drugs. What else could he be?"

Vinnie was getting pretty fucking tired of Juicy and the other Golden Griddle waitresses always going on about the writer-guy. At least that's what Geordie, the alternate night-cook, said he was. Geordie had asked or something.

The writer-guy was always scribbling in a green leather book. He used a fountain pen, too, a black one with a French name. Juicy's sister Jen, who was a bus-girl on weekend nights, couldn't remember what type of pen it was, just that it was expensive. Jen said that was the sure sign he was a queer. A normal guy, according to Jen, would have used a ball-point. *Jesus Christ*, thought Vinnie miserably, *what a couple of inbreeds.*

Vinnie had been planning his escape from the town since he was fourteen. And here he was, almost nineteen, still working at the Golden Griddle in the Milton Mall. If there was a God, he was deaf to all of Vinnie's prayers, and had been for years.

"What are you?" giggled Juicy inanely. "His bum-chum? You wanna date him, Vinnie? I bet he likes you. He's always tellin' me, 'Oh *do* give my compliments to the chef,' like he's never had fuckin' *chicken* before in his life, and he says it all fruity." Juicy convulsed with laughter. "Hey, Jason!" she screamed to the dishwasher, who looked pleased to be included in the conversation. People called Jason a retard, and said he did steroids. He laughed, low and idiotic, waiting for Juicy to go on. "I think our Vinnie-boy has a mystery side," Juicy said coyly.

Jason, who had taken a puck to the head when he was twelve—at least that's what everyone said—grinned expectantly. He rarely understood jokes without having them explained to him. Juicy knew this, and didn't explain. She tittered behind her hand and turned away from Jason.

"Fuck off, Juicy," Vinnie snapped. "You're getting fuckin' fat, you know that? Too many deep-fried chicken wings at Jukebox Charlie's for you." He laughed, and pointed to her huge ass. "You got a rip along the crack of them dress pants."

Juicy gasped and blanched. She craned her neck, fingering the back of her pants, looking desperately for the rip in the burgundy polyester waitress slacks.

"Where? Where?" she shrieked. "Vinnie, where?" She did a little dance, looking for the rip. "Are you lyin'?" she asked suspiciously. "Okay, what color underwears am I wearin'?"

"Pink, with white stripes," jeered Vinnie. "Every night's Wing Night for Juicy. Lard-ass night, more likely."

"Liar, I am not! My underwears are *white!* There's no fuckin' rip."

She snatched the writer-guy's chicken (broiled, without the skin, as per his request—another sure sign, according to Jen) from under the heat lamp, and flounced toward the door. She turned around and smirked at Vinnie one last time. "Are you *sure* you don't wanna take this plate out to him yourself, Vinnie?" she whispered coyly, batting her eyelashes. "Seein' as though you two are *such* good buddies?" She pushed open the door and carried the plate to the writer-guy. Vinnie knew she'd be perfectly polite. She always was, to people's faces.

Vinnie walked across the greasy floor to the door and peered through the window into the dining room at Juicy and the writer guy. Juicy was tossing her home-permed red hair and smiling at him, proba-bly asking personal questions and inventing answers that she could use later. The writer-guy was smiling up at her, polite as could be, but a little reserved. Juicy, with her red hair, red face, and burgundy Golden Griddle uniform, looked like a scarlet whoopie cushion. The writer-guy, in con-trast, was smooth-skinned and pale, with high cheekbones. He had dark brown hair, almost black, and dark eyes, and looked to Vinnie to be about thirty. He wore gray flannel slacks and a blue button-down. His tweed jacket hung over the back of his chair. He carried a battered brown leather briefcase. Vinnie thought he looked very civilized. Smart too, like a professor.

He sighed, and went to scrape the grill, vaguely wondering what the writer-guy was putting in the green leather book, wondering if he was writing about him, or Juicy, or the town. He hoped that Juicy wouldn't scare him off. He'd like to talk to the guy sometime. He'd like to ask the guy what the *fuck* he was doing in Milton, Ontario at nine o'clock on a Friday night, eating alone at the Golden Griddle restaurant. Somehow he thought that the writer-guy might understand a thing or two about want-ing to get out of Milton, even if he *had* moved here of his own free will.

AT one o'clock in the morning, Vinnie turned off the lights of the restaurant, set the alarm, and locked the door. Juicy had left at midnight. Not a moment too soon, thought Vinnie, who'd felt that he might have to bash her one in the head with the frying pan if she didn't stop razzing him about the writer-guy.

Vinnie stepped out into the cold night air of the parking lot. The streetlights were shrouded by a curtain of snow, falling swiftly and silently, muffling all sound except the fierce wind. Vinnie pulled up the collar of his black leather biker jacket, and walked carefully across the lot to where his burgundy '79 Cutlass Supreme was parked. The pavement was black ice beneath the snow, and he'd already taken a particularly painful pratfall the previous week. His bruises were yellowing, but it had hurt like hell. He had to open the restaurant tomorrow morning. He couldn't do it from a hospital bed. The managers were tit-useless, always arriving late and leaving early, patting themselves on the back if the evening had gone well, blaming him and Juicy if it hadn't.

His car was covered in snow. Vinnie brushed off the windshield as best he could with he sleeve of his leather jacket, then unlocked his car and stepped into the frigid interior. He turned the key in the ignition and turned the heat up, rubbing his hands to warm them. When the car was sufficiently heated, he drove out of the Milton Mall parking lot and turned left on Main Street, guiding the car carefully through the blizzard. The snow danced in the car's headlights, making Vinnie's head ache. He'd been driving for ten minutes by the time he passed the Little Caesar's pizza place and the Shoppers Drug Mart, just before the intersection of Main and Martin, a jaunt that would have taken him maybe three minutes in less inclement weather. A flurry of motion out the left window suddenly caught his eye, and instinctively he put his foot to the brake, bringing the car skidding to a full stop in front of the Moviola Cafe. The snow was blowing like God's own bitch, and Vinnie craned his neck forward to see out of the windshield. As he stared, he heard a high, keening wail that wasn't the wind, and a stumbling black shape separated itself from the howling wildness of the snowstorm. It fell once, then stood up and righted itself, arms outstretched. It threw back its head, and Vinnie could see blue eyes crazed with terror and agony streaming tears that froze as quickly as they fell. Something like the high collar of a dark fur coat obscured most of the figure's face. When Vinnie, alarmed, called out "Hey! Are you okay?" he saw who it was.

Juicy lurched toward him, frantically clawing something away from her face that Vinnie first took to be a dark, tattered scarf. He saw her mouth open then, and she shrieked, peal after peal. Juicy fell again, a few yards away from where Vinnie stood. Her screams were abruptly cut off as the discarded scarf suddenly twisted on the ground, and surged greedily toward her exposed face and mouth. The darkness divided, uniting with the seething mass of blackness that swarmed all over her body.

Juicy was crawling with rats. They swarmed over her in a filthy pulsating mass, tangling in her hair, scrabbling eagerly over her face, hanging by sharp yellow teeth to her sleeves, burrowing into her shredded winter coat.

Their eyes glittered like tiny rubies in the car's headlights. Vinnie heard the squeaking and saw that the rats numbered in the thousands. They swept across the snow like an oily stain, streaming across the snowdrifts from under houses and buildings and out of the trash dumpsters behind the Moviola. A tidal wave of them surged toward Juicy from across the frozen millpond bordered by Rotary Park across the street. They fell on her from the roofs of the shops along Main Street, tangling in her red hair, squealing eagerly as they sought out her exposed face and hands, biting her viciously when she tried to brush them away.

Juicy tried to scream again, and a rat scrabbled up her chin and nudged its head into her open mouth.

I am not fucking seeing this, thought Vinnie wildly as his gorge rose. His brain tried vainly to process the impossibility. There is no fucking way this is happening. He tasted bile in the back of his throat.

Juicy stretched out her fingers to Vinnie in mute supplication. As he stared, dazzled by horror, an enormous brown rat poked its head out of Juicy's sleeve and scuttled across her hand. It sat on the snowbank and glared balefully at Vinnie. Its whiskers twitched as it bared its jagged yellow teeth. It chattered angrily and charged. Vinnie screamed and lashed out with his booted foot. He heard a sickening crunch as his boot connected with the rat's head, breaking its neck as it smashed against the passenger-side door of the Cutlass.

He stumbled backward. Turning his head away from Juicy and the rats, he vomited on the snow. The smell of it reached him almost instantly, and Vinnie heaved again and again, the sound of his retching mingling with Juicy's shrill screams, weaker now, and the music of the rats. Then suddenly, there was silence.

Vinnie wiped his mouth with the back of his hand and turned toward Juicy. She was huddled in a fetal position. She wasn't moving. The army of rats had circled her prone body and given it a wide berth. They crowded together, not moving, rank on rank. Their eyes were trained on Vinnie, and their whiskers twitched impatiently as though waiting for some command that only they could hear.

Something fluttered heavily in the air above Vinnie's head, something that sounded huge. Vinnie turned his head toward the sound, and caught a glimpse of a soaring shadow that swept down from the night sky into the shadows of the alley behind the Moviola Cafe.

"Why did you stop to look, little brother?"

The voice drifted like mist from the alleyway. It was the most beautiful man's voice that Vinnie had ever heard. It coursed like a river of cool silver into his ears. Dimly he became aware that he had an erection. His knees buckled, and he slipped on the snow. Vinnie saw the armada of rats as though from a great distance.

"Why did you have to see?" That voice again, like a caress. "There was nothing here for you to see. She would have been nothing to us."

Struggling to his knees, Vinnie realized he had stretched out his arms toward the alleyway. He lost his balance and fell again. He thought he heard the man's soft laughter.

The world is waiting, Vinnie thought. The rats were forgotten. Juicy was forgotten. The tropical sun shone brightly and the snow blew pink and warm. Vinnie felt himself lifted up and borne on warm currents of silver water. He closed his eyes and felt the hot sun on his face. He was floating. His erection throbbed, and his nipples were taut and aching under his shirt. From another galaxy he heard his mother ask him if he wanted some fresh lemonade, and if he did, come out of the water and get it himself. Endless, endless summer days.

Vinnie opened his eyes. The blowing curtain of snow parted as the tall man in black stepped out of the shadows. He was over six feet tall, with wide shoulders and white-blond cropped hair. He wore a black leather jacket with silver-studded epaulets into which were tucked a pair of heavy black gloves. His skintight black leather pants, laced along the outer thigh, were tucked into heavy black boots. Powerful leg muscles flexed and strained as he walked slowly over to where Vinnie lay shivering on the on the ground. Bending down on one knee, the man in black brought his face down so it was level with Vinnie's.

He's good lookin', thought Vinnie crazily, and at that moment he knew that he wanted the man to kiss him.

"Do you want to know something secret about your friend Juicy before you both die?" he whispered. It sounded like the most marvelous idea that Vinnie had ever heard.

"Yeah..." Vinnie breathed.

The man brushed his cold lips against Vinnie's forehead. "She has a runaway mouth. And I'm not as forgiving as my lover."

The lips caressed his cheek, and he felt the man's tongue exploring the inside of his ear. *I'm bein' kissed by a guy*, Vinnie thought dreamily. *It feels so fuckin' good. Uh-oh. What if Juicy sees me and tells everybody I'm a big fag?* And then Vinnie remembered the rats.

"I'm not a big fan of gossips, as you might have noticed. Especially this stupid redheaded cunt. Rumors always seem to get back to the person being gossiped about, don't they? In this case, me."

"Who are you?" muttered Vinnie sleepily. His lips were beginning to freeze, and the snowflakes were coating his eyelashes, making it difficult to keep his eyes open. Light danced at the edge of his sight, and when he tried to focus on the dark figure hovering above him, he saw purple and black flowers blossom in front of his eyes.

"Who *am* I? Come *on*, small-town boy." The man's voice flowed like dark music. "Even a stinking backwoods hick like you ought to be smarter than that. Who do you think I am?"

The man's face was pale as bleached bone. His eyes shone like flickering points of fire rimmed with silver. As Vinnie stared, he opened his mouth, and Vinnie saw the dripping fangs.

"What do you call him in that kitchen of yours, behind his back when you think he can't hear you? 'That queer?' The 'writer-guy'? Well, I'm the writer-guy's 'kissing cousin,' as Juicy the brainless fucking squat of a waitress explained to you a few hours ago, before she became food for the gods. That's who I am."

Vinnie's sigh caught in his throat as the fire smoldering in the blond man's gaze suddenly exploded. His eyes became blazing twin suns streaming red light across the darkness of space. Vinnie felt the man's tapered fingers open his jacket and pull down the collar of his turtleneck.

Aching with love, his erection pounding painfully inside his jeans, Vinnie arched his back and stretched his throat upward. The man licked his lips and lowered his mouth to Vinnie's jugular. Vinnie felt cool breath on his neck, and the stinging pain of two sharp teeth on the tender skin of his throat. He closed his eyes in ecstasy, waiting.

Vinnie heard a sound like thunder, felt a sudden blast of icy air, and then there was no one straddling him. His mind was cloudy with images of brilliant crimson planets detonating against a vast nebula of limitless blackness. Dully, Vinnie rolled his head toward the cacophony of snarls, crashes and screams which had erupted just out of his line of sight. He tried to call out irritably that he wanted his kiss, had been promised it in fact, but his vocal chords were paralyzed. Vinnie could only roll his head. He was unable to move his arms and legs.

And then he saw. Vinnie's eyes widened as his sanity struggled to reconcile what he was seeing with what he knew the parameters of reality could possibly be. The blond man was playing on the snow with what looked like a large timber wolf. They rolled and thrashed on the ground, kicking up clumps of snow as they played.

But no, they weren't playing at all. The wolf had its jaws clamped on the blond man's throat. The blond man was ripping and punching, screaming, but not in fear. To Vinnie, he seemed far beyond anger, far beyond even rage. He attacked the wolf with redoubled fury, gaining a momentary advantage. The wolf's jaws clamped down on the epaulet of the blond man's leather jacket, and tore away a chunk of shoulder. Black blood erupted from the tattered mass of bone and torn muscle. The blond man shrieked in agony, and clutched his mangled shoulder. But instead of drawing back, he bared his fangs and sank them into the wolf's matted coat. They rolled across the parking lot, leaving a trail of steaming blood from their wounds on the snow.

Then, as Vinnie watched, the figure of the blond man appeared to dissolve, becoming a sparkling silver-blue fog that spiraled upward into the night. The wolf reared up on its hind legs and snapped furiously at the spinning mist. The mist darkened and elongated, and Vinnie had the brief impression of black fur and angry red eyes hovering in the air above him. The blond man's voice ricocheted into his brain like a whip, full of hate and pain and thwarted rage.

Soon, motherfucker.

Then the air was full of the sound of leathery wings beating furiously in the whirling snow. Vinnie felt a blast of icy wind as something swept up into the air and streaked into the night sky in the direction of Martin Street.

Vinnie heard a low growl. The wolf padded silently toward where he lay, still paralyzed. The blood was already vanishing beneath a pristine layer of freshly-fallen snow. The wolf's muzzle was clotted with gore. He watched in horror as the wolf approached his supine body and lay down on

top of him. Unable to move, unable to scream, he could only watch help-
lessly as the beast began to lick his throat. The wolf began to pant, its massive flanks shuddering with excitement. Vinnie felt hot breath on his face,
and the acrid smell was like blood and pennies. The wolf began to whine
and growl softly. When Vinnie saw the sharp white teeth dripping with
saliva in the gaping red maw, he knew he was going to die. He closed his
eyes, hoping his impending death would hurt less if he couldn't see it. The
wolf's rough tongue continued to lap at his throat.

Open your eyes.

Vinnie obeyed the voice that insinuated itself suddenly into the violent miasma of thoughts and images flooding his brain. The wolf was staring down at him. It was no longer panting or whining. Its heavy body felt
warm and comforting. Images of his father carrying him up to bed after
he'd fallen asleep in front of the Christmas tree when he was four years old
flickered across the screen behind his eyes.

Vinnie stared back, because he knew that was what he was supposed to do.

As he watched, the wolf's eyes began to glow with the sullen glare of
red fire, but there was no answering terror in him. Vinnie tried to draw
closer to the warmth, but couldn't move. The two flaming eyes came
closer.

Flowers of pure silver erupted in the midst of the red. Vinnie
watched, fascinated, as the silver spilled out across the snow, bathing him
in warmth. The sweet silver became his whole world, and he felt his eyelids
flickering again, becoming heavier than he had ever felt them.

Sleep, murmured the soothing, cultured voice in his head.

Vinnie's last coherent thought before the silver and red darkness
bore him up was that the voice in his head reminded him of someone he'd
known in a life light-years before this nightmare of rats and monsters and
wolves. Oddly, it sounded like the sort of suggestion the writer-guy might
have made. The idea was so reasonable, so civilized.

Yes, sleep was the thing. When he woke up again, none of this would
be real. Juicy should have just shut up, thought Vinnie, then none of this
would have happened.

ANGRY voices intruded on Vinnie's dreams. His parents were arguing again.

It must be morning, but he felt as though he hadn't slept at all. Every muscle in his body ached and his head was pounding. He moaned softly and burrowed his face in the pillow.

The angry voices continued, the verbal duelists thrusting and parrying, taking no prisoners, seeking out vulnerabilities and submerged resentments as only the long-married can. But this time it was about Vinnie.

Something about...what? His curfew? Something Vinnie had watched on television?

"...never take responsibility for anything...let him see...could have been trouble..."

"...didn't want to move here...damned kid...us....don't belong here..."

"...always have to have the last word...just give a little for once in your overly-long life..."

Something about Vinnie. There was going to be hell to pay when he got up and went down to breakfast, he could tell by the way their voices rose and fell. God, they had been married for so fucking long, you'd have thought they'd have run out of things to fight about. Vinnie wasn't ever going to get married.

And then:

"...stupid little bitch should have kept her mouth shut..."

"...my problem, not yours. Who cares what they think anyway? Why don't you let me handle the townspeople my way, and save the Fright Night theatrics for your concerts...."

Vinnie's eyes snapped open, and he sat bolt upright, fully awake.

He wasn't at home, he was lying on a gold and red sofa in a room with pale white walls and high ceilings. The only light in the room came from dozens of silver candelabra placed around the room. Flowers, mostly red and white roses, were artfully arranged in heavy cut-crystal vases. The candles' glow caught the refracting edges of the vases, scattering the light like a shower of diamonds. A fire crackled in the white marble fireplace across the room. The carpet covering the gleaming hardwood floors was Oriental in design, intricate weavings of gold and burgundy geometric shapes. He swung his legs over the side of the couch and kicked the heavy fur throw off his legs. His mind was cloudy, and his head ached. The ghost memory of his dream drifted on the edges of his consciousness. Something about snow, and Juicy, and...rats? But if he wasn't at home, who had been arguing? Or was that part of the dream, too?

Where the *fuck* was he? Vinnie had never seen a room like this anywhere in Milton. Even when some of his friends' mothers took it into their heads to "redecorate," as they always called it, this usually meant buying uncomfortable white wicker furniture and painting the walls peach, or steam-cleaning the wall-to-wall carpet, or pasting baby-chicken printed wallpaper in the kitchen.

This furniture was gleaming antique mahogany, burnished to a glossy red patina. The scent of lemon oil and potpourri lingered in the air. The bookshelves overflowed with books, hundreds of them, and for a moment he doubted that he was in Milton at all.

From another room came the sound of a classical piano piece. Mozart, thought Vinnie, but then everything classical sounded to him like Mozart, at least if it didn't have words. If it had words, and they were in Italian, he knew that it was opera. Vinnie hated opera. He explored the room on tiptoes, pausing in front of the fire. Above the mantelpiece, along which were lined several smaller votive candles in delicate porcelain dishes, a large portrait in oils dominated the room. Vinnie had seen paintings like it in history books. The figure sitting on the dark-rose damask chair in the portrait looked familiar, but he couldn't place it. And then it came to him. It was the writer-guy. Or maybe the writer-guy's...grandfather? The painting seemed to be from another century.

Realization hit him. He knew where he was. The old red house on Martin Street. The writer-guy's house.

"Oh look, our boy's awake."

The voice, still beautiful, was cold and mocking. The blond man stood in the doorway, wearing his leather pants and nothing else. The pants were torn and shredded. His chest and arms were heavily muscled. The skin was pale and smooth, as though it hadn't ever seen the sun. The writer-guy stood behind him. Vinnie hadn't heard either of them enter the room.

"Marcus, *please!*" urged the writer-guy. "Give the kid a break." Turning to Vinnie, he said, "I'm terribly sorry about all this. We couldn't take you back to your mother's house and just leave you there in a basket with a note pinned to your jacket like Oliver Twist, and we could hardly leave you in the snow."

He slipped one arm around the blond man's waist, and laid his head on his shoulder. The blond man yelped and drew back.

"Damn it! Watch yourself! The shoulder isn't healed yet!"

"You're usually tougher than that, Marcus." He turned to Vinnie and said, "Well, in all fairness, I like it when he's tough."

The writer guy smiled. Vinnie caught firelight gleaming off the writer-guy's canine teeth, and his nightmare came crashing back to him. It had all been real, then. Everything. His knees wobbled, and he leaned against the arm of the sofa for support.

"You fucking bit half my arm off back there," growled the blond man, Marcus. He continued to ignore Vinnie. "Easy, would you?"

"Marcus," his friend remonstrated. "I wish you'd watch your language. Vinnie is a guest in our home. He'll think we're savages. Vinnie, we've never actually been formally introduced. My name is Charles Webster. I've enjoyed your cooking so much during my gastronomic peregrinations at the Golden Griddle." Webster extended his hand to Vinnie, who stared at it mutely. Webster glanced briefly at Marcus. He raised one eyebrow, and smoothly retracted his hand.

"Charles, for God's sake," snapped Marcus. "Even I have a hard time following what you say when you talk like that."

"Sorry," Webster said. "You know me and language. Sometimes I get carried away." Indicating the blond man, he said, "This is my...friend, Baron Marcus. Ignore the title, we usually do. It's very old—Prussian, actually—but Marcus has long since lost his accent, and this sweet little town isn't really the place for accents or titles of nobility, is it?"

"Uh," said Vinnie.

"Naturally," Webster beamed. "Any sensible person would agree. But as I was saying, please excuse Marcus' half-undressed state. He had a little accident tonight." Webster smiled conspiratorially at Marcus as though trying to engage him in a private joke. Marcus sulked, glowering at Webster .

"What happened?" Vinnie asked fearfully.

"A wolf bit him," Webster replied.

"You guys *live* together?" stuttered Vinnie. He pointed to Marcus. "That guy...he..."

"You mean Marcus?" said Webster smoothly.

"Yeah," Vinnie gasped. "He's not your cousin?"

"No, he's not."

"Are you guys like...do you have *wives?*"

"No, we don't."

Webster looked amused. Marcus looked bored. The supercilious eyes of the portrait above the mantelpiece looked down at Vinnie with contempt.

"Girlfriends?" muttered Vinnie weakly. "Do you guys have, like, girlfriends?"

"No!" snapped Marcus. "Jesus Christ, Charles! Why do we have to answer this little fucker's questions? I say we waste him now, and send him off to join that little bitch waitress friend of his."

Drugs, thought Vinnie. *Juicy was right. They're a couple of queer drug dealers And they've killed Juicy, because she discovered their secret.*

"Marcus! Calm yourself please. No one's going to 'waste' anyone. Vinnie, would you like a cup of tea or something? You look a trifle pale."

"No, I don't want *tea!*" blustered Vinnie. If he was going to get out of this house alive, he was going to have to make these two psycho faggots believe he wasn't afraid of them. He felt his bowels churning. "You guys aren't cousins at all. You're two guys livin' together in this house. You don't have wives, or even girlfriends. Jesus Christ! All the stories were true. Juicy was right! You guys are a couple of—"

"Vampires," finished Marcus. "We're vampires."

"Bullshit!" screamed Vinnie. "You're just a coupla fags!"

"Oh, dear me, no," Webster chuckled. "Well, we're that too, of course. Marcus *is* my lover, and we've been together for a very long time. But 'just a couple of fags?' Ah, would that it were that simple." He sighed delicately and ran his long white fingers along the inside of Marcus' torn leather pants.

"Now we *have* to kill him," hissed Marcus, advancing on Vinnie. His canine and incisors were lengthening. His eyes began to glow.

"Marcus," said Webster irritably. "Stop it right now."

Marcus glared at his lover. Resentfully, he obliged. His teeth returned to their normal size, and his eyes became clear blue again.

"This isn't the way to do things," explained Webster. "This is Milton, Ontario, Marcus, a tiny little hamlet off Canada's longest highway. The McDonald's sign on highway 401—that's what this town *is*. Milton has a metropolitan population of thirty thousand people, and yet somehow they all seem to goddamn well *know* one another. He'd be missed. And besides, these people already suspect that we're different from them. Killing him won't make it any easier for us to blend in and keep a low profile."

Blend in, thought Vinnie desperately. *Keep a low profile? Not in this lifetime.* "The disappearance of that little slut Juicy is going to cause some talk as it is. I do wish you'd been able to control your passions, Marcus," he chided. "They'll be the undoing of us one of these days."

Vinnie began to weep. "I don't wanna know this stuff," Vinnie cried. "Just let me go, please! I wanna go home!"

"There, there," soothed Webster. "No need to cry." He pulled a lace handkerchief out of his pocket. The handkerchief was monogrammed C.M.W. It was flecked with brown spots of dried blood. "We moved here for peace and quiet, that's all. Well, I moved here for peace and quiet anyway. I am a writer, of sorts, Juicy had that part right. Marcus fronts an alternative musical group on Queen Street, in Toronto. A Goth band," Webster explained sourly. "Oh, if only they knew. But I digress. Marcus moved here rather against his will, under considerable duress. He did it for me, because he loves me. Marcus, though, is less tolerant than I am. Hence, the unpleasantness with the rats tonight."

"You shouldn't have stopped me, Charles!" Marcus spat. "No one would have found her body! And we'd have one less yakking cunt spreading stories about us."

Webster patted Marcus' hand indulgently. "As our kind go, Marcus is very young. As for me," he shrugged, "I've lived a long, long time, and I've gotten used to a lot more than he has."

"We didn't do nothin' to you," Vinnie sobbed. "We just left you alone and let you do what you wanted. You come into the Griddle with normal people and eat your chicken and nobody ever bothers you. Juicy talked about you, yeah sure, but she talks about everybody. Yeah, she called you a fag, but that doesn't mean anything. It's just a word. It was just talk."

"Well now," said Webster, smiling thinly. "It would appear that we have different standards of acceptable behavior. Without putting too fine a point on it, Marcus and I really are different from you and your kind. In spite of what you may have read about us in popular journals and reviews, it all has less to do with living what we've heard described as"—and here the vampire laughed softly—"an 'alternative lifestyle' than it does with being, well, better. A different species. Vastly superior. We are the aristocrats of this world, Vinnie. Its stewards. We've given human society much more than it has ever given us—art, culture, literature."

"Tout-petit Levi's cutoffs worn with Doc Martens," snickered Marcus. "Leather chaps. Disco, too, if you trace it right back to Europe in 1974."

Webster shot him a withering glance. "We were poets and kings and warriors," continued Webster implacably. "The history books are full of the contributions of our kind. Most of the credit has gone to others, alas, but that's to be expected given the times in which they lived. The dishonesty has to do with the Church, for the most part. Most true evil does. But we do demand respect on behalf of those of us who've gone before. It's a matter of pride."

Webster smiled, and walked over to the portrait above the mantelpiece.

I've lived a long, long time.

"I daresay we're very sensitive, Marcus and I," he sighed. "My lover is far more physical than I am, far more prone to violence. Tonight I had to stop him from tearing you apart. It wouldn't have done us any good, you know. Still, we're aware of being gossiped about, and it irritates us. And whatever my own personal feelings about your death, or Juicy's for that matter, as an aristocrat Marcus has the right to end your life if it occurs to him. It is natural that his wish that you die take precedence over your wish that you live."

"I don't want to die," whimpered Vinnie. "Please, don't let him get me."

"You're quite safe at the moment, Vinnie," said Webster. "I give you my word.

"How did you know about all the talk?" Vinnie sniffled, wiping his face with the bloody handkerchief. "Nobody never said nothing in front of you."

"We hear things," Webster said. "You'd be surprised what we can do. Our minds roam, even when we're asleep in our coffins." He winked at Vinnie. "It's true about the coffins. You know that don't you? They're in the basement. Would you like to go downstairs and see?"

Vinnie shook his head violently.

"Oh yes," said Webster. "We can go anywhere, see anything. Your dirty little secrets are nothing to us." The vampire closed his eyes. "I can travel thousands of miles without moving a muscle. I can even travel to your house. Right into your mother's *bedroom*...she's dreaming about you right now, did you know that? She fell asleep at exactly one o'clock, and her last thought before she drifted off was that the weather was bad, and she hoped you'd drive safely." Webster opened his eyes and wagged his index finger at Vinnie.

"You *wicked* boy! Did you really steal the family car when you were fifteen in order to go over to some little tramp's house in Campbelville, then wreck it? Your mother has never forgiven you for violating her trust that way, you know. She remembers it every time you aren't home exactly on time."

The vampire's eyes gleamed. "She's terribly afraid for you, Vinnie," he confided. "You're so irresponsible. On some level she's always prepared for you to die on the highway. Especially on a cold winter night like this one, when the snow is so bad.

"Oh, Vinnie," he murmured sadly, "why did you have to stop the car tonight? Things were going so well for us here in this town."

He turned toward Marcus who was slouched in the doorway, arms crossed over his chest. Webster wore a look of resignation. "I fear your first impulse may have been the correct one, my love. This may have gone too far."

"Please," whispered Vinnie. "Please let me go. I won't say nothing, I swear."

"No, I know you won't," mused Webster. "But not for the reasons you think."

"What happened to Juicy?" Vinnie mumbled, stalling.

Keep them talking. Keep them busy. Try to make them forget that I know their secret. I never wanted to know it! I never wanted to do anything but leave this town! They can do what they want to in the privacy of their own homes. It's none of my business. It's nobody's business! But oh, God, Jesus, let me get out of here alive.

"You'll find her somewhat...changed," said Webster with dark humor.

The vampire smiled and stretched out his long white fingers. A cool wind sighed through the room, and the flames of the candles flickered and went out. The only light in the room came from the fire in the grate, now burning low and blue. Tendrils of mist rose from the bodies of Webster and Marcus.

Marcus' voice was like jagged ice in a frozen graveyard. "You'll be seeing her very soon. In fact, I think you're going to be spending a fair bit of time together in the next little while. And with us, too, of course. This house is enormous."

"Don't!" Vinnie gibbered. "Please! I want my mother!"

"Slaughtering you would be so easy," Webster said wistfully. "My strong Marcus would love to do it himself. But it would be too messy and there would be too much in the way of explanations. No, better that you disappear for three nights." The vampire winked lewdly. "Maybe they'll think you're shacked up with that little beaver of yours in Campbelville, eh? You *stallion*, you! And then," Webster said mockingly, "in three nights—the same time it took Our Lord to tunnel his way out of his grave like a rat—you can visit your mother in the darkness of her bedroom while she lies dreaming, and you can kiss her."

Webster turned abruptly to Marcus and dragged a sharp thumbnail across his muscular chest, cutting the nipple in half. Blood erupted from the cut. Vinnie heard a sharp intake of breath, but Marcus placed his hands behind his head, back ramrod straight, eyes forward. He presented his chest to Webster as though inviting a further test of his endurance. Webster licked the trickle that spurted from the wound. His eyes rolled back in his head and he groaned in ecstasy at the communion. Marcus stood unflinching. As Vinnie watched, Webster's teeth grew longer and sharper. His lips were stained red with his lover's blood.

Miraculously, before Vinnie's eyes, the cut healed itself. The nipple became whole, the pectoral became smooth and unblemished once again. Webster turned back to Vinnie, smiling faintly. Marcus placed his powerful arm protectively around Webster's shoulder. He stared defiantly at Vinnie.

"We have so much to teach you," Webster continued, leaning into the shelter of Marcus' massive body. "Your friend Juicy will have to learn a little more in the way of tolerance. Marcus isn't a very patient teacher, and some lessons can be quite painful."

"Please," pleaded Vinnie. "I stuck up for you! I told them that you were a regular guy! I told them to leave you alone! I just wanted to talk to you!"

"And I appreciate your intervention, Vinnie, I truly do. Alas," he sighed, "it was a case of too little too late. But don't worry, we'll have many, many nights to talk. We're going to be good friends, you and I."

Webster and Marcus drifted toward him. Vinnie closed his eyes, and thought about the first time he'd heard Marcus' ebony voice in the swirling snow, felt himself become hard and aching at the cold touch of Marcus' fingers. *Maybe it won't hurt,* he thought to himself. *Maybe I could get to like it.*

He felt strong hands on either shoulder, felt icy fingers entwine gently in his hair. He felt cool breath on his neck, and he smelled musk.

Now I'm never going to get out of this town, Vinnie thought. *Never, ever.*

"Oh, but you're so wrong about that," he heard Webster whisper. "You're so, so wrong. You'll go everywhere. There is so much of the world to see. As the centuries pass, you'll acquire the powers of a god. And when the hunger comes to you, Vinnie, you'll turn to your own kind for the love you need."

Vinnie felt two sets of fangs slice effortlessly through the soft flesh of his throat, and he understood. There was only momentary pain, then heat. Then nothing but an eternity of nights stretching out in front of him like a ribbon of lightless highway.

As the darkness came to call, Vinnie felt the vampires gather his body in their arms, cradling him gently so he wouldn't fall as they fed.

BOARD CENTER
4 CAR TRAIN

THOMAS S. ROCHE

THE train burst into the station, screaming. Fluorescence washed over me. I shivered but stood my ground and put my shades on.

The wind was like a hurricane. I crouched where the rats hide, in the hollow next to the track, among the Super Big Gulp cups and discarded newspapers, spent 9mm shell casings and those sticks from ice cream bars. Then the train was past me, and its shadow shielded me from the station lights as I crouched next to the track.

BOARD CENTER 4 CAR TRAIN

The screens forced the point, again and again, giving orders but not making much sense. I watched as the train groaned to a halt. I could hear the voices of the people commuting late at night. People who worked night jobs—hookers, drug dealers, bus drivers, store clerks, boywhores, security guards, serial killers, haunted men and women. Their voices formed together in a chant.

COLMA

BOARD CENTER 4 CAR TRAIN

BOARD CENTER 4 CAR TRAIN

BOARD CENTER 4 CAR TRAIN

The train pulled smoothly out of the station again. Anticipating the light, I ducked into the tunnel and was gone.

The hunger was terrible inside me. People didn't come down here much anymore, and I had been slowly starving, day by day, week by week, growing weaker and closer to the final death. As the city above decayed, the residents hung their fears on the underground world, and avoided it. It wasn't such a bad idea.

I made my way back to the hollow where I'd hidden my last victim, a homeless punk boy who had wandered into the underworld and who had shrieked as he died. I said prayers over his body wishing for some sort of absolution, the repose of his soul or mine, either or preferably both. I sucked on his dried bones, hoping to find some speck of marrow, some kind of nourishment—but there was none. Angrily, I crunched the bones in my teeth. I breathed hard as I scattered the bones like leaves and walked deeper under the city.

I had only been window-shopping. I would have to be an idiot to seek satisfaction in an underground terminal; the security guards wore black ballistic clothing and carried Mini-Uzis, Mac-10s, AKs, M-16s. And with enough rounds per minute one of them might get lucky and sever my spine or hit me square in the forehead before I tore her or his throat out and scattered blood across ballistic cloth. It was too risky to hunt in the station. I had only been dreaming—dreaming of blood.

✳ ✳ ✳

The sound of footsteps made me turn, and I saw Adam. I had grown so lonely in the weeks since I'd seen him. But my hunger was stronger than my loneliness, which it always had been. I raised my hand, motioning him away. My hunger was such that I could not trust myself. In this state I couldn't control my need—and maybe he couldn't either. Even so I felt an ache and longed to embrace him. A flood of memories washed over me— the first time we shot up together, the first time we drank each others' blood...the first time we hunted, after the change had come over us—then he took a step closer.

"Stay back!" I hissed. Adam crouched, about ten feet from me. Rats ran past his booted feet. Adam was youthful vigor and fifteen-year-old beauty gone corrupt and desiccated with a hundred years of track marks and infected abscesses. Still he was lovely. I looked at the blue veins beneath the paper-thin skin of his cheeks, the deep, mourning black eyes, the subtle poetry of his black hair in the breeze from the tunnel. The slope of his pulsing throat...my lips drew back, sharp fangs ready—

"Stay there!" I growled at him. "Stay where you are!"

There was the faraway sound of a stray cat in heat, howling.

Adam's eyes blossomed sad and moist.

He was very weak, so weak his hunger seemed to be fading. I knew from the cast of his skin that Adam was feeding about as often as I was, maybe less. His arms had grown thin and bony since I saw him last. The ancient marks lining each arm had begun once again to abscess. I knew he was very sick and it pained me to see him lapsing. I knew it couldn't be long, for either of us.

Strands of his black hair scattered on the wind. His blood-red lips were taking on shades of purple. His dime-store jewelry hung loosely on his wrists and neck, and his combat boots were worn through. The tattered remains of his Chem Lab T-shirt were beginning to dissolve into threads, revealing the sharp bones of his ribs. I had shoplifted that T-shirt for him as a present at the sleazy head shop down on Market, stuffing it down my pants and slipping out the door while the cracked-out biker at the counter was eyeballing some punk broad. In happier times.

Adam stared at me for a long time, shaking.

"I haven't seen you...." he said. His words came out in a forlorn sort of moan. "I've started to really miss you—"

"I can't trust either of us," I spat. Adam seemed to be going delirious with hunger. "We're both so fucking hungry. We can't get too close...."

"Oh God, I'm hungry...."

His fingers had lost most of the skull and eyeball and snake rings. Adam started to sway. I fought down a wave of terrible hunger as I moved to catch him. Trembling, I brought him down and laid him gently on the soft ground. My belly ached. It would be so easy to open up his throat with my fangs and drink him—

Instead, I ran my fingers through his hair, fighting down wave after wave of the insane need which almost drove me to destroy him.

"They don't come down here anymore," I rasped. "Some of us were careless...we gave ourselves away. The surface people are afraid. They know we're down here."

"They'll come down to get us...?"

"Soon," I told him.

"I can't wait," he moaned softly. "I've got to go up there and—"

"Adam! Don't even fucking consider it!"

"But I'm so hungry...."

"I mean it! If you go out there you're dead! You know that! It's not just the light! It's a fucking nightmare out there! The gangs have SWAT teams for breakfast and fucking Green Berets for lunch! This town is a slaughterhouse—you have to wait for them to come down here!"

"I know, I know. *I know.*" His head lolled back, and his white throat was exposed—

Barely able to see straight, I reached back and fished the straight razor out of my pocket. Adam was almost unconscious. It was all I could do to keep from devouring him. I shut my eyes and forced myself to think of other things: the taste of his lips, the blossom of Adam's blood in a syringe—

I felt sure that I had eaten more recently than Adam. I couldn't let him die like this—

Gently, I drew the straight razor across the palm of my hand. Slowly, beads of blood formed.

Adam's lips were slightly parted. I held my palm over his mouth, letting the beads form—

One drop.

Adam's eyes brightened. His breath came more quickly. His lips parted wider.

Two.

Light seemed to glow in his eyes. His tongue lolled out.

More.

Strength flowed tangibly through him. I squeezed my hand at the base, working out another droplet—

Then one hand was at my throat, yanking me down, the other hand grasping my wrist. The straight razor slipped from my sweat-slick fingers. A hunting wail filled my ears, a psychotic scream. I tried to push away but before I could counterhold he had me on my back and his fangs, filmed with blood, were descending—

"No! Adam—"

I reached desperately for the razor, searching for it on the concrete floor. Adam was aware of nothing but his desire to feed on me. I felt his hard, lithe body pressed against mine, holding me down. He was delirious, murderous, with desire. I screamed for mercy and felt his iron arms going around me, forcing me down, as he wrestled me under him and fitted fangs into my throat—

I felt the razor, got it by the handle.

Adam screamed as I dragged the blade across his cheek. It gave me the moment I needed to get my knee under him and slam it into his crotch. Breathless, he landed on his ass and I came down on him, hard, slashing across his throat. Blood sprayed across my hands and face. I didn't cut him deep enough to kill him, more out of accident than design. I lifted the razor to bring down the killing stroke, overwhelmed with hunger. Then I found my mouth on his throat, suckling, the guttural growl deep in my throat. The strength went out of his limbs and I felt him succumbing, surrendering, as he had so often, as I said, in happier times.

I pulled myself away, choking on his blood. I couldn't feed on him like this. I couldn't.

We were both covered in blood, but Adam had lost more of it than me. I began to crawl away. He groped for a handhold on my ankle, but I kicked his shoulder, hard, and his grip weakened. I crawled away and left Adam there, bleeding.

I struggled to my feet. He was too weak to rise, and his blood darkened the tunnel's floor.

"Yves—" he rasped. "Forgive me—"

"Fuck off," I said, tasting my own tears and blood. I stumbled down the corridor, the straight razor slick with blood in my hand.

ADAM'S blood sustained me for a time, but as the need came again I wished I'd drunk it all. I wandered through the empty tunnels smelling dead rats and feces, tasting bile, clawing at my own scarred chest through what remained of the Motorhead T-shirt Adam had snagged from the booth at Shoreline for me. I could feel the need so acute in my throat and belly.

I slept under a pile of bones and, unable to control myself, killed a rat, which did nothing for my hunger but just made me crave the good stuff that much more. I lay there moaning through the day and most of the night. The need passed with a shudder, but I knew it would return.

It occurred to me that Adam's blood had tasted so different the night I'd first taken it in his apartment, back when he lived on fourteenth Street...back when I didn't know what was happening to our bodies.

When I was able to move without taxing myself too much, I wandered through the darker caverns, through the oldest and foulest of the sewers and transit tubes. Some of these had never been used; they were built and then abandoned.

I found myself in an area I had never seen before, but I knew from the smell of rotting fish and chemicals and raw sewage that I was close to the bay. There was an exit somewhere. The fresh air burned in my lungs. It seemed like it would be so easy to slip out of the tunnels, to find a victim among those in the city—maybe by the waterfront.

No! It was too dangerous. That was how Jason had died, and Diane and the others....

Biting my lip, hard, I walked toward the exit. I saw a shadow. I felt my lips twist, but I wasn't sure whether I was supposed to be smiling or snarling.

The faintest stream of moonlight came through and hit my face. I muttered a line from an insipid early-eighties pop song and put on my shades.

BLUE nightmare. It had all been an escape, of sorts, an adventure. It was cheap on the street, especially if you got it from the guy on Capp who muttered "Nightmares, nightmares, nightmares," or the diesel dykes running the auto shop on Shotwell by the projects. It was the seeds of some obscure Brazilian flower, the blood of an Egyptian snake, the roots of a Tibetan tree, the testes of Komodo dragons—the stories varied. The high was like the release after waking from a nightmare (hence the name), pure rush and desperate happiness, insight, sudden terrified understanding—no comedown and no fucking hangover. Blue nightmare was the newest thing in the midnight clubs, and I helped to put it there. I knew this guy with Peruvian connections who supplied me with nightmare dimebags I paid for with cash advances from dad's credit cards. Soon I had a nice little operation going, dealing to my friends. I guess I was some sort of a fucking big shot for a while—you see, the first one's always free.

I never used large quantities of the drug at one time—not as much as Andrew, or Rija or the others. I never got really high for very long, and I never binged. That's why it took me longer to succumb to its effects. Adam used less than I did, but not by much. I think I felt what was happening before he did, felt the flesh of my upper lips contracting, felt the paper-dry texture of my flesh when I pushed the needle in. I think I heard, in my blue-nightmare stupor, the howling of demons.

I guess the blood was my idea. Adam had loved it, being an old deathrocker by heart. It was better than sex—far better than sex—and neither of us quite knew what we were playing with or understood that this just wasn't some fucking game, that it wasn't a coincidence that we were sharing blood.

I wasn't surprised when my friends started disappearing. You sort of expect it nowadays, at least if you ever watch the evening news or read the papers.

By then it was too late, and we were all too far gone. There's no such thing as withdrawal from the nightmare. You just don't get out.

Adam vanished one night. It was my birthday. We'd spent the afternoon fucking and bleeding for each other, we had some nightmare, and then in the evening we laid around on the bed wrapped up in the torn sheets, watching the tape of old Nick Cave videos he'd snagged for our anniversary from the music and porno shop on Hyde while the tranny clerk traded waxing tips with a Latino boywhore. I fell asleep watching "From Her to Eternity" and dreamed of Saint Nick murdering thirteen-year-old boys somewhere in Alabama. I woke up from the nightmare shaking, the TV spitting white noise and snow at me. I lay there lonely, like a little kid, wondering why he'd left me, why I was alone. Things started to sort out in my brain. I started to feel the pangs, a craving in my bones. I think I just sort of realized all of a sudden what the fuck was going on here.

Now I knew why I was alone, and where Adam had gone. He'd gone *down*.

And things were totally fucked.

I dragged the TV into the windowless living room and slept all day, having more nightmares about Trent Reznor eviscerating me with a rotary saw. Overnight and all the next day I went cold turkey from blue nightmare, and when I awoke at dusk with the sun smearing its blood-red fingers across the horizon, I tasted the tang at the back of my mouth and felt every cell in my body screaming in demon-voices for the drug. But I knew I would never again have the nightmare, for the fucking dream had been made flesh.

As I crawled through the apartment, the setting sun came through the bedroom window and made my skin wither, blister; thin trails of smoke came off of me and rose to the ceiling. The fresh air from the open window ate my lungs. Moaning, I scrambled out of the bedroom, crawled through piles of fast-food wrappers and dirty underwear, closed the window and the black-velvet curtains, and lay there running my tongue over my canines. They were half an inch longer than they'd been when I passed out.

Closing my eyes, tasting my feral need, I began to moan, low in my throat. A rank scent seemed to seep through the walls. I heard gunfire outside.

In the city, downwind from the cemeteries, The gutters were filled with broken glass....

ADAM'S body was destroyed, his face a mask of fear, remorse, and razor-slashes. It must have been horrible to die alone.

His eyes were wide open; he was doubled over, his hands were claws from raking the broken concrete, desperately reaching for nourishment as the last blood flowed out of him. His stomach, concave, his tongue and lips swollen, the flesh of his cheek and throat destroyed by the slash of the razor and the brutal rip of my teeth. He had died screaming.

Hating myself for it, I desperately put my mouth to his throat and drank. There was nothing. He had been dead too long.

I took him in my arms as I sucked at his flesh, biting in, receiving nothing. He had wanted to devour me. Now he would never devour anyone. I rose, reached out and closed his eyes.

I looked at the tunnel floor, where he'd scribed what might have passed for a suicide note in different circumstances.

His death would haunt me, I knew.

I built him a cairn of concrete chunks and broken glass, and laid him out in the sewer tunnels by the ocean. I could smell the salt, its tang like a dangerous seduction toward running water. His tombstone was a plywood board. I wrote his name on it with a big marker I'd taken months ago off an unfortunate punk scrawling graffiti in a sewer tunnel. I made the "A" in his name into an anarchy symbol, like he used to do when he signed his notes to me. It didn't really fit any more but what the fuck, he would have appreciated it.

Crossing his hands over his breast, I wept a silent liturgy, a vampiric eulogy. I muttered prayers to a dark god whose name had not yet been spoken. Had I been able, I would have shed a tear.

Adam went to sleep and left my world. I turned, and left him in the darkness.

PERHAPS his death haunted me more than it would have, had he not scribed "Sorry Yves too Hungry Love Sorry" with an old piece of chalk on the tunnel floor. For a while after that I couldn't stop crying as I wandered through the tunnels. I'm a sentimental fucker at heart, in case you haven't fucking noticed. That was the last thing I expected. It read like a Hallmark card from hell.

I WANDERED, lost, for a long time after Adam's death, not sure what was flowing through my veins. Was it Adam's beautiful soul, which I had loved so much, or the poison of betrayal, which I had also loved in a way? The straight razor came to my throat many times as I wandered in the dark, but I never had the balls to make the cut, partially because I couldn't bear to let Adam's blood flow again. Like I said, I'm a sentimental fucker, much to my own recurrent dismay.

IT seemed like I hadn't heard human sobbing in years. I generally moved too fast to elicit that response from my victims—and of course, I was unable, since that evening when I first awoke, to weep.

I melted into the shadows, moving without making a sound.

Her smell was overpowering. I could hardly stop from moaning my need. I watched her as the faint light played over her. She was right by the opening. The moonlight lit her bleach-white hair on fire. She wore a leather jacket with skulls painted all over it, and silver skulls hung from her ears. Her skin had gone white, but the transformation was not yet complete. She still lived. Her black miniskirt showed track marks across the back of her thighs. She wore a black Lycia T-shirt that had been torn open, and a tattoo of a human heart, dripping blood, was visible on her left breast.

She stood squarely in the shaft of moonlight. The light came from a sewer grate, telling me that outside, even in the middle of the night, was death in flames. *Starry Night* in acetylene and black velvet. The electric lights couldn't kill like that, but the light of the sun, even reflected from the moon, and even the light of the distant stars, could blister my flesh in seconds. I could not go to her, not in my weakened state. The light was too much. If only she would come out of the light, I could take her.

The girl was smoking a cigarette. She kept choking and spitting, as if there were a bad taste in her mouth.

She was sobbing. Her body was wracked by some horrible pain. I recognized the stance, the look of her crumbling, brittle hair, the paleness of her skin.

She turned, suddenly, and saw me. She yelped momentarily. I should have taken that moment to leap, but I could not brave the moonlight.

I crouched in the dark tunnel, unmoving.

"You scared me," she said faintly.

"Sorry," I said.

"I'm not doing so well...you going to hurt me?"

"No," I lied.

"I'm really not doing so well," she repeated, swaying, like she needed someone to talk to. "I...I do too many drugs."

"Me too," I told her sadly.

"Right. I know." She laughed nervously. "Doesn't everyone. But...I'm hooked...and then I was fixing up, and suddenly...well, maybe I got a bad batch or something. I started getting all weird, hearing these voices...and other stuff, and I got these shakes all over, like I was having convulsions...." She had trouble pronouncing "convulsions"—she was slurring her words. "They fired me from this job—I worked at this club. It was kind of a...gentleman's club, you know? Me and my girlfriend, we were gonna move to Phoenix soon as I got the money together. I hear it's really cool down there, you can live cheap and there's lots of awesome people, not like here." A look of fear and confusion twisted her face. "But I guess that's all over now. She and me...."

"Fuck," I said, my voice shaking. "That's rough."

"Yeah, you know? It really fucking is. One day you just fucking wake up and you don't have anything to say to someone anymore. I mean, or maybe, maybe, maybe this is it, maybe you fucking have lots to say to them, like everything in the fucking world you want to say to them, but, you know, you don't fucking know how to say it, like you want to, you want to—or maybe she can't say it to you or something, what it is she wants to say— fuck I don't know—" She looked down and put her hand over her eyes.

Her white throat glistened in the shaft of moonlight. Fuck, I couldn't do this. This was like killing a crying child. Even Saint Nick would have backed off from this one. The hunger crumbled in an instant and I felt myself dying inside. It had seemed different with Adam. But maybe I had already signed my death certificate when I gave enough of a shit about him to hold off on ripping his throat out, and now I was just sticking around to rot. When the craving goes, the craving to feed above all else, then you should really just bend over and kiss your ass goodbye.

She was sobbing uncontrollably, choking on cigarette smoke, her mascara smeared across her cheeks. I sat down on the rocks facing her, spent.

"Man," I said. "That's harsh."

"It sucks," she told me. "Life fucking sucks."

"No shit," I said.

"Yeah," she said. "It does. It really really does. You know, it all started when I fucking got canned for like no reason. Everyone passed the nightmare around, but I got caught by the owner one day and they just fucking dumped me like I was some junkie or something. It was total bullshit. The guy was an asshole. He wouldn't even listen to me. That's when I really got into the stuff, you know, I didn't have anything better to do. I had money, I'd been saving it, but I just didn't care enough any more. All 'cause I lost this stupid job which was bullshit in the first place. I mean, guys all over you, and everything smells like Clorox...." Her tears had stopped, and now she looked angry. She lit another cigarette from the butt of the first one.

She went on. "It was like I couldn't handle the drug anymore. I couldn't stand it. I thought I was going to explode. I thought I would die. Every time I shot it I thought I was going to go crazy. It scared me. Do you think I caught something bad? I never shared needles...."

She crushed out her cigarette, which she didn't seem to be enjoying anyway.

"Maybe. Maybe you caught something. Like from a bad batch or something."

Her eyes went wide. "I hope it's nothing that's going to hurt me...."

I didn't say anything.

"You know what I heard," she said, softly, her voice cracking. "Someone told me that they take the night out of the brains of mental patients, ones with a certain condition. People who go really crazy. That there's some factory in Argentina where they keep them all tied up and keep their brains producing the drug. Or something. This guy I was seeing told me that a long time ago. Before I ever did it. I think he was just trying to freak me out." She made a disgusted sound. "He was a real asshole. I hope I'm not gonna die from whatever it is. I always told myself I'd get off drugs some day."

"You will," I said vaguely.

She breathed deep. She crossed her arms across her chest.

"Good," she sighed. "I'm really afraid. I feel...like I want another fix, but I'm afraid to...."

I pictured her, running in the tunnels, hiding in the shadows, feeding on security guards, screaming and moaning for food when the victims were few, covered with blood when they were many. I saw her years of agony, of watching friends starve to death as I had watched Adam, of suffering with the rats and the filth and aching, aching, always aching for nourishment.

"I can't seem to stand the light," she said. "Even at night. Even the moonlight hurts my eyes. My skin feels all prickly." She put up her hand to block out the moonlight. "It's almost dawn. I can't stand the thought of going out into the sun. It's been so hot lately. Even with the fog. It's so weird how it's so hot in the winter, isn't it? Even when it's foggy? God, it's fucking bright in here."

"Come out of the light, then," I said, aching.

It was as if, in that moment, she sensed instinctively what was coming.

"You're not going to hurt me?"

I shrugged. "Who knows?"

She took a few steps toward me, but didn't quite step out of the shaft of moonlight She seemed to sense something was wrong, but lacked the will to run. On the other hand, maybe she trusted me.

"It wouldn't be so bad living down here...though I'd kind of miss my brother, I suppose. But he doesn't really want to see me any more. He just keeps trying to get me into rehab. I mean, he's got his little house in the Castro, you know, on the other side of the gate, with his boyfriend and all his stereo equipment, and he doesn't want to deal with me, it's like I'm his family secret." Her face twisted again, more horribly this time. "But I'd still miss him, if I went away." She squinted at me. "I guess I still love him, even if he's my brother. Hey, do people live down here?"

"Yeah."

"How come? I mean, with the fucking rents, it kinda makes sense. They just like it down here?"

"Uh...it's a very long story."

"Well, I have time."

I paused. I felt a sadness. I stepped toward her, and she gasped. She took a step back, away from me, and came out of the shaft of moonlight. I began to circle toward her, around the light.

She did not move away. Just stared, as if she finally understood. As if she had laid her eyes upon a true brother. One who wouldn't try to put her in rehab. A brother of the fucking night.

"What's your name?" I asked her.

"Nightmare," she said, and I was unclear as to whether that was really her name, or she had just misunderstood the question. Not that it mattered. Nightmare, then.

She did not scream, but only gasped as she went down. I held her hair, knotted in my fist, so that her head would remain at the proper angle, and opened up her throat. Her eyes went wide as I descended.

"I'm sorry, Nightmare." I whispered it like a chant into her throat, dribbles of blood running over my hands. "But this, as you so eloquently put it, is bullshit."

Her body jerked, spasmed; she erupted in a thick stream down my throat. She began to wail, softly, but it was not the wail of a victim. It was a sound of release, of freedom. Her mouth opened and her tongue popped out.

I took her in my arms for the last moment of her life, and placed a drop of blood on her tongue with mine.

"What the fuck...?" she whispered as she failed.

"I'm sorry," I told her, but I wasn't sure if I really was, or had merely misunderstood the question.

My mouth descended again, and her tattoo became a geyser. I clutched her tight until she was empty, her body thin and brittle.

I licked my lips and my fingers. I picked up Nightmare's desiccated remains and carried her deep into the tunnels. I was very strong now. I looked into her open eyes as I walked. Even in death they were very sad.

I passed Adam's cairn, and the many piles of bones where I or others had left victims previously. I normally did not do what I was about to. But somehow I had to, for Nightmare, for the girl.

I made my way to the last train line that was still running. I found my way to the edge of the station. I kept my shades on as I squinted into the light. It hurt like hell.

I brushed her hair back, looking at her face. Better she should die than live this life, fleeing from the headlights of trains and eating rats. Better that her life should end in a violent embrace than in a low, lingering death in the sewers that could last for ten thousand years. And better I should feed. Who the fuck was I to play judge, jury, and executioner down here in the sewers? This was the law of the jungle, and for me to plead love for the human race was like some sort of moral version of Tourette's syndrome. I knew, and I hated myself for it, that in the end I had taken Nightmare only, or mostly, because of my hunger. Anything else I felt—any mercy, any sympathy, any regret—was so much conspicuous and fragrant bullshit.

The headlights of the train appeared. Their heat burned me. There was a loud electronic wail, the scream of technology's cathartic arrival—

BAY POINT

BOARD CENTER 4 CAR TRAIN

BOARD CENTER 4 CAR TRAIN

BOARD CENTER 4 CAR TRAIN

BOARD CENTER 4 CAR TRAIN

The train burst into the station, screaming, and Nightmare leapt, or was pushed. She struck the train in an angel's pose, and the driver screamed and ducked. Nightmare exploded.

Her ex-girlfriend would cry, her brother would mourn her passing, and they would both have something to bury. They would be able to explain the unfortunate suicide of a sister and lover; they would recall her descent into madness and talk about how they had tried to help, and blame her death on misfortune, and hide themselves, however unsuccessfuly, from its shadow. They would mutter blasphemous twelve-step prayers and would never know the truth, or the possibilities.

BAY POINT

BOARD CENTER 4 CAR TRAIN

BOARD CENTER 4 CAR TRAIN

BOARD CENTER 4 CAR TRAIN

FREMONT AND RICHMOND LINES

TRANSFER AT 12TH STREET STATION

I ducked into blackness, as the screams erupted from whores, junkies, security guards. My sins were now someone else's problem.

I would return to my dark world and one day soon a living victim would come to me and I would take him or her, and my death would continue for another ten thousand years. But Nightmare's death had been accomplished in an instant, a beautiful instant that carried with it a hellish closure, so at least I could console myself that I had provided three seconds of brutal mercy—however unjust and unasked-for that mercy might have been.

This was more than I had done for Adam, who had died badly.

I went to the place near the water where Adam would sleep forever, or until they decided to build a new subway tunnel, and offered his dead lips a drop of blood from my fingertips. It was too late—it always had been—but I thought he would appreciate the gesture. I lay there and imagined we were waking up early in our flat on Florida, with the sound of dealers and cops in the alley outside, with the bright blessing of a brutal sunrise streaming slanted light onto the bed, ruining all our nightmares and scattering gold in Adam's hair. It was dawn.

THE MAUSOLEUM: NOTES ON THE CONTRIBUTORS

Bruce Benderson is the author of the critically acclaimed novel *User*, about street hustlers in Times Square, and the short story collection *Pretending to Say No*. He lives in New York.

Michael Thomas Ford is the author of numerous books, including *The World Out There*, *OutSpoken*, and *If Jesus Loves Me, Why Hasn't He Called?* His fiction and essays have appeared in magazines such as *Paramour*, *Cupido*, and *Starphkr*, and in anthologies including *Best American Erotica* 1995 and 1997 and the *Flesh and the Word* series. He lives in Boston.

Caitlín R. Kiernan was born near Dublin, Ireland, but has lived most of her life in the southeastern United States. Her short stories have appeared in numerous anthologies, including *High Fantastic*, *Dark Terrors 2*, *Darkside: Horror for the Next Millenium*, *Love in Vein 2*, *Lethal Kisses*, and *Sandman: Book of Dreams*. She is the author of a novel, *Silk*, Caitlín lives in Athens, Georgia, where she divides her time between writing and her band, Death's Little Sister.

Kevin Andrew Murphy is a widely anthologized author of dark satire, horror, and fantasy whose work has appeared in the magazines *Permission* and *Verotika*, and in such anthologies as *The King is Dead* and *Splatterpunks 2*, among others. He is the co-author of the novel *House of Secrets* and the author of *Penny Dreadful*.

Award-winning film and television writer/director **Ron Oliver** is the only person living in his West Hollywood neighborhood who actually owns a leopard skin suit. He is currently single and can usually be found under the pool table at the Motherlode Bar on Santa Monica Boulevard. Fan mail and pronouncements of love can be sent to ROliver588@aol.com.

David Quinn, one of the premiere creators of the early nineties "Outlaw Comics" movement, is best known for *Faust: Love of the Damned*, a serial graphic novel he continues to produce in collaboration with artist Tim Vigil. The penultimate chapter will appear later this year, along with editions in English, French, and Italian.

Simon Sheppard's work has appeared in many anthologies, including *Best American Erotica 1997, Best Gay Erotica 1996* and *1997, Grave Passions: Stories of the Gay Supernatural, Bending the Landscape: Fantasy, Eros Ex Machina*, and *Noirotica* and *Noirotica 2*. He would like to acknowledge the invaluable assistance of Leo Enzlin's Amsterdam Retreat for Wayward Writers.

Robert Thomson is the author of *Secret Things* and *Signs of Life*. His fiction and journalism have appeared in *Queer View Mirror 1* and *2, Happily Ever After: Erotic Fairy Tales for Men, The James White Review, XTRA West!, fab, The Scream Factory*, and *Icon*. Robert lives in Toronto and is the managing editor of *FAB National* magazine.

Edo van Belkom made an auspicious debut in the horror field when his first short story "Baseball Memories" was reprinted in *Year's Best Horror Stories 20*. Since then, he has published over one hundred stories of science fiction, fantasy, horror and mystery to magazines and anthologies such as *Palace Corbie, Haunts, On Spec, Northern Frights, Shock Rock 2, Fear Itself, Hot Blood 6, Dark Destiny, Seductive Spectres, Demon Sex*, and *Robert Bloch's Psychos*. His first novel, *WyrmWolf*, was a finalist for the Horror Writers Association 1995 Bram Stoker Award for Superior Achievement in a First Novel. Other novels include *Lord Soth, Army of the Dead*, and *Mister Magick*.

ABOUT THE EDITORS

Michael Rowe is a widely anthologized writer, journalist, and essayist, and co-editor (with Thomas S. Roche) of the vampire anthology *Sons of Darkness: Tales of Men, Blood and Immortality* (Cleis Press, 1996). His first collection of interviews, *Writing Below The Belt: Conversations With Erotic Authors*, was published in 1995 by Richard Kasak Books. His second collection, *Voices: Conversations With Gay and Lesbian Authors*, is forthcoming from Richard Kasak Books in 1998, as is his first novel. He is senior writer of FAB National magazine in Toronto, where he lives with his life partner, Brian McDermid.

Thomas S. Roche is a writer, performer, and editor whose more than one hundred short stories and essays have appeared in magazines such as *Black Sheets*, *Blue Blood*, *Cupido*, and *Paramour*, and in such anthologies as *Best American Erotica 1996* and *1997*, *Best Gay Erotica 1996*, and *The Mammoth Book of Pulp Fiction*, among many others. Previous anthologies he has edited or co-edited include *Noirotica* and *Noirotica 2*, *Sons of Darkness*, and *Gargoyles*. Some of his short fiction is collected in *Dark Matter* (Masquerade Books, 1997). He lives in San Francisco.

VAMPS:
An Illustrated History of the Femme Fatale
By Pam Keesey

According to popular vampirologist Pam Keesey, all bad girls can trace their origins to the vampire, that quintessential evil woman who uses sex as a weapon. From Greta Garbo to Sharon Stone, these irresistible women are seen as creatures of great appetites who step outside the realm of acceptable feminine behavior to satisfy their desires.

Vamps: An Illustrated History of the Femme Fatale presents riveting images of women as predators, from ancient goddesses and witches to the vamps of the silver screen. Keesey's fascinating cultural history is punctuated by excerpts of interviews with film stars and critics. This book is a must-buy for vampire lovers and movie fans who treasure images of women as powerful, sexual beings. Over 100 photographs of favorite film "vamps" — Joan Crawford, Faye Dunaway, Theda Bara, Greta Garbo, Marlene Dietrich, Sharon Stone, Catherine Deneuve, Tallulah Bankhead, Mae West, Gloria Swanson, Betty Boop.

"If you have a vagina and a point of view, that's a deadly combination." — Sharon Stone.

$21.95   ISBN: 1-57344-026-4

Call to order:
Cleis Press 1-800-780-2279

POPULAR LESBIAN VAMPIRE TALES FROM PAM KEESEY

Dark Angels and Daughters of Darkness, Pam Keesey's bestselling lesbian vampire collections, feature the quintessential bad girls, archetypes of passion and terror. Guaranteed to get under your skin, piercing with tales of desire so sharply erotic you'll swear you've been bitten!

Daughters of Darkness
Edited by Pam Keesey
Features Katherine V. Forrest, Pat Califia, Jewelle Gomez, Robbi Sommers—as well as the most famous lesbian vampire story of all time, "Carmilla," written in 1871 by J. Sheridan LeFanu.
Bibliography and filmography
$12.95   ISBN: 0-939416-78-6

"Perfect for curling up on dark and stormy winter nights..."—The Rocket

Dark Angels
Lesbian Vampire Stories
Edited by Pam Keesey
Amelia G, Gary Bowen, Melanie Tem, Cora Linn Daniels, Carol Leonard, Lawrence Schimel, Cecilia Tan, Thomas S. Roche, Renee Charles, Alejandra Pizarnik, Shawn Dell.
$10.95   ISBN: 1-57344-014-0

ALSO: Keesey's irresistible collection of tales of ferocious women...

Women Who Run with the Werewolves
Tales of Blood, Lust and Metamorphosis
Edited by Pam Keesey
Like the vampire, the female werewolf is dangerous and alluring, using her sexuality to destroy men. But while the vampire employs seduction to capture her prey, the female werewolf is most often associated with raw lust and animal instinct. Her desire literally turns her into an animal. When she takes her sexuality into her own hands, she becomes a killer.
Ursula LeGuin, Suzy McKee Charnas, Amelia G., Thomas Roche, Lawrence Schimel, Charlee Jacob, Melanie Tem, Lawrence Schimel, Thomas Roche, Tom Piccirilli
$12.95   ISBN: 1-57344-057-4

Call to order:
Cleis Press 1-800-780-2279

Books from Cleis Press

EROTIC LITERATURE

Best Gay Erotica 1998, selected by Christopher Bram, edited by Richard Labonté.
ISBN: 1-57344-031-0 14.95 paper.

Best Gay Erotica 1997, selected by Douglas Sadownick, edited by Richard Labonté.
ISBN: 1-57344-067-1 14.95 paper.

Best Gay Erotica 1996, selected by Scott Heim, edited by Michael Ford.
ISBN: 1-57344-052-3 12.95 paper.

Best Lesbian Erotica 1998, selected by Jenifer Levin, edited by Tristan Taormino.
ISBN: 1-57344-032-9 14.95 paper.

Best Lesbian Erotica 1997, selected by Jewelle Gomez, edited by Tristan Taormino.
ISBN: 1-57344-065-5 14.95 paper.

Serious Pleasure: Lesbian Erotic Stories and Poetry, edited by the Sheba Collective.
ISBN: 0-939416-45-X 9.95 paper.

GENDER TRANSGRESSION

Body Alchemy: Transsexual Portraits by Loren Cameron. Lambda Literary Award Winner. ISBN: 1-57344-062-0 24.95 paper.

Dagger: On Butch Women, edited by Roxxie, Lily Burana, Linnea Due.
ISBN: 0-939416-82-4 14.95 paper.

I Am My Own Woman: The Outlaw Life of Charlotte von Mahlsdorf, translated by Jean Hollander.
ISBN: 1-57344-010-8 12.95 paper.

PoMoSexuals: Challenging Assumptions about Gender and Sexuality edited by Carol Queen and Lawrence Schimel. Preface by Kate Bornstein.
ISBN: 1-57344-074-4 14.95 paper.

Sex Changes: The Politics of Transgenderism by Pat Califia.
ISBN: 1-57344-072-8 16.95 paper.

Switch Hitters: Lesbians Write Gay Male Erotica and Gay Men Write Lesbian Erotica, edited by Carol Queen and Lawrence Schimel. ISBN: 1-57344-021-3 12.95 paper.

SEXUAL POLITICS

Forbidden Passages: Writings Banned in Canada, introductions by Pat Califia and Janine Fuller. Lambda Literary Award Winner. ISBN: 1-57344-019-1 14.95 paper.

Public Sex: The Culture of Radical Sex by Pat Califia.
ISBN: 0-939416-89-1 12.95 paper.

Real Live Nude Girl: Chronicles of Sex-Positive Culture by Carol Queen.
ISBN: 1-57344-073-6. 14.95 paper.

Sex Work: Writings by Women in the Sex Industry, edited by Frédérique Delacoste and Priscilla Alexander.
ISBN: 0-939416-11-5 16.95 paper.

Susie Bright's Sexual Reality: A Virtual Sex World Reader by Susie Bright.
ISBN: 0-939416-59-X 9.95 paper.

Susie Bright's Sexwise by Susie Bright.
ISBN: 1-57344-002-7 10.95 paper.

Susie Sexpert's Lesbian Sex World by Susie Bright. ISBN: 0-939416-35-2 9.95 paper.

LESBIAN AND GAY STUDIES

The Case of the Good-For-Nothing Girlfriend by Mabel Maney. Lambda Literary Award Nominee.
ISBN: 0-939416-91-3 10.95 paper.

The Case of the Not-So-Nice Nurse by Mabel Maney. Lambda Literary Award Nominee. ISBN: 0-939416-76-X 9.95 paper.

Nancy Clue and the Hardly Boys in A Ghost in the Closet by Mabel Maney. Lambda Literary Award Nominee.
ISBN: 1-57344-012-4 10.95 paper.

Different Daughters: A Book by Mothers of Lesbians, second edition, edited by Louise Rafkin. ISBN: 1-57344-050-7 12.95 paper.

Different Mothers: Sons & Daughters of Lesbians Talk about Their Lives, edited by Louise Rafkin. Lambda Literary Award Winner. ISBN: 0-939416-41-7 9.95 paper.

A Lesbian Love Advisor by Celeste West. ISBN: 0-939416-26-3 9.95 paper.

On the Rails: A Memoir, second edition, by Linda Niemann. Introduction by Leslie Marmon Silko. ISBN: 1-57344-064-7. 14.95 paper.

Queer Dog: Homo Pup Poetry, edited by Gerry Gomez Pearlberg. ISBN: 1-57344-071-X. 12.95. paper.

SEX GUIDES

Good Sex: Real Stories from Real People, second edition, by Julia Hutton. ISBN: 1-57344-000-0 14.95 paper.

The New Good Vibrations Guide to Sex: Tips and techniques from America's favorite sex-toy store, second edition, by Cathy Winks and Anne Semans. ISBN: 1-57344-069-8 21.95 paper.

The Ultimate Guide to Anal Sex for Women by Tristan Taormino. ISBN: 1-57344-028-0 14.95 paper.

DEBUT FICTION

Memory Mambo by Achy Obejas. Lambda Literary Award Winner. ISBN: 1-57344-017-5 12.95 paper.

We Came All The Way from Cuba So You Could Dress Like This?: Stories by Achy Obejas. Lambda Literary Award Nominee. ISBN: 0-939416-93-X 10.95 paper.

Seeing Dell by Carol Guess ISBN: 1-57344-023-X 12.95 paper.

WORLD LITERATURE

A Forbidden Passion by Cristina Peri Rossi. ISBN: 0-939416-68-9 9.95 paper.

Half a Revolution: Contemporary Fiction by Russian Women, edited by Masha Gessen. ISBN: 1-57344-006-X $12.95 paper.

The Little School: Tales of Disappearance and Survival in Argentina by Alicia Partnoy. ISBN: 0-939416-07-7 9.95 paper.

Peggy Deery: An Irish Family at War by Nell McCafferty. ISBN: 0-939416-39-5 9.95 paper.

THRILLERS & DYSTOPIAS

Another Love by Erzsébet Galgóczi. ISBN: 0-939416-51-4 8.95 paper.

Dirty Weekend: A Novel of Revenge by Helen Zahavi. ISBN: 0-939416-85-9 10.95 paper.

Only Lawyers Dancing by Jan McKemmish. ISBN: 0-939416-69-7 9.95 paper.

The Wall by Marlen Haushofer. ISBN: 0-939416-54-9 9.95 paper.

VAMPIRES & HORROR

Brothers of the Night: Gay Vampire Stories edited by Michael Rowe and Thomas S. Roche. ISBN: 1-57344-025-6 14.95 paper.

Dark Angels: Lesbian Vampire Stories, edited by Pam Keesey. Lambda Literary Award Nominee. ISBN: 1-7344-014-0 10.95 paper.

Daughters of Darkness: Lesbian Vampire Stories, edited by Pam Keesey. ISBN: 0-939416-78-6 9.95 paper.

Vamps: An Illustrtated History of the Femme Fatale by Pam Keesey. ISBN: 1-57344-026-4 21.95.

Sons of Darkness: Tales of Men, Blood and Immortality, edited by Michael Rowe and Thomas S. Roche. Lambda Literary Award Nominee. ISBN: 1-57344-059-0 12.95 paper.

Women Who Run with the Werewolves: Tales of Blood, Lust and Metamorphosis, edited by Pam Keesey. Lambda Literary Award Nominee.
ISBN: 1-57344-057-4 12.95 paper.

POLITICS OF HEALTH

The Absence of the Dead Is Their Way of Appearing by Mary Winfrey Trautmann.
ISBN: 0-939416-04-2 8.95 paper.

Don't: A Woman's Word by Elly Danica.
ISBN: 0-939416-22-0 8.95 paper

Voices in the Night: Women Speaking About Incest, edited by Toni A.H. McNaron and Yarrow Morgan.
ISBN: 0-939416-02-6 9.95 paper.

With the Power of Each Breath: A Disabled Women's Anthology, edited by Susan Browne, Debra Connors and Nanci Stern.
ISBN: 0-939416-06-9 10.95 paper.

COMIX

Dyke Strippers: Lesbian Cartoonists A to Z, edited by Roz Warren.
ISBN: 1-57344-008-6 16.95 paper.

The Night Audrey's Vibrator Spoke: A Stonewall Riots Collection by Andrea Natalie. Lambda Literary Award Nominee.
ISBN: 0-939416-64-6 8.95 paper.

Revenge of Hothead Paisan: Homicidal Lesbian Terrorist by Diane DiMassa. Lambda Literary Award Nominee.
ISBN: 1-57344-016-7 16.95 paper.

TRAVEL & COOKING

Betty and Pansy's Severe Queer Review of New York by Betty Pearl and Pansy.
ISBN: 1-57344-070-1 10.95 paper.

Betty and Pansy's Severe Queer Review of San Francisco by Betty Pearl and Pansy.
ISBN: 1-57344-056-6 10.95 paper.

Food for Life & Other Dish, edited by Lawrence Schimel.
ISBN: 1-57344-061-2 14.95 paper.

WRITER'S REFERENCE

Putting Out: The Essential Publishing Resource Guide For Gay and Lesbian Writers, fourth edition, by Edisol W. Dotson.
ISBN: 1-57344-033-7 14.95 paper.

Since 1980, Cleis Press has published provocative, smart books—for girlfriends of all genders. Cleis Press books are easy to find at your favorite bookstore—or direct from us! We welcome your order and will ship your books as quickly as possible. Individual orders must be prepaid (U.S. dollars only). Please add 15% shipping. CA residents add 8.5% sales tax. MasterCard and Visa orders: include account number, exp. date, and signature.

How to Order

• **Phone:** 1-800-780-2279 or (415) 575-4700
Monday–Friday, 9 am–5 pm Pacific Standard Time

• **Fax:** (415) 575-4705

• **Mail:** Cleis Press P.O. Box 14684, San Francisco, California 94114

• **E-mail:** Cleis@aol.com